At Devlin's question, Liz pulled in another breath. She could think of a hundred reasons to refuse his request. She didn't really know this man, wasn't sure she believed everything he'd told her.

Yet she couldn't deny he acted on her like a damn spark plug. Every time he got this close, he transmitted an electrical energy that made her pulse rev faster and her skin get hotter. Still, she was pretty sure she would have denied his request if the rig had remained stable.

Well, It didn't pitch much. Just enough to send Liz staggering forward a step, smack into Devlin's denim-covered chest.

"I'll take that as a yes," he said, his voice edged with a husky note that had Liz's toes curling into the deck.

Dear Reader,

Thanks for choosing Silhouette Desire this month. We have a delectable selection of reads for you to enjoy, beginning with our newest installment of THE ELLIOTTS. *Mr. and Mistress* by Heidi Betts is the story of millionaire Cullen Elliott and his mistress who is desperately trying to hide her unexpected pregnancy. Also out this month is the second book of Maureen Child's SUMMER OF SECRETS. *Strictly Lonergan's Business* is a boss/assistant book that will delight you all the way through to its wonderful conclusion.

We are launching a brand-new continuity series this month with SECRET LIVES OF SOCIETY WIVES. The debut title, *The Rags-To-Riches Wife* by Metsy Hingle, tells the story of a working-class woman who has a night of passion with a millionaire and then gets blackmailed into becoming his wife.

We have much more in store for you this month, including Merline Lovelace's *Devlin and the Deep Blue Sea,* part of her cross-line series, CODE NAME: DANGER, in which a feisty female pilot becomes embroiled in a passionate, dangerous relationship. Brenda Jackson is back with a new unforgettable Westmoreland male, in *The Durango Affair.* And Kristi Gold launches a three-book thematic promotion about RICH AND RECLUSIVE men, with *House of Midnight Fantasies.*

Please enjoy all the wonderful books we have for you this month in Silhouette Desire.

Happy reading,

Melissa Jeglinski

Melissa Jeglinski
Senior Editor
Silhouette Books

Please address questions and book requests to:
Silhouette Reader Service
U.S.: 3010 Walden Ave., P.O. Box 1325, Buffalo, NY 14269
Canadian: P.O. Box 609, Fort Erie, Ont. L2A 5X3

MERLINE LOVELACE

Devlin and the Deep Blue Sea

Silhouette®

Desire

Published by Silhouette Books

America's Publisher of Contemporary Romance

SILHOUETTE BOOKS

ISBN 0-373-76726-9

DEVLIN AND THE DEEP BLUE SEA

Copyright © 2006 by Merline Lovelace

This edition published by arrangement with Harlequin Books S.A.

® and TM are trademarks of Harlequin Books S.A., used under license. Trademarks indicated with ® are registered in the United States Patent and Trademark Office, the Canadian Trade Marks Office and in other countries.

Visit Silhouette Books at www.eHarlequin.com

Printed in U.S.A.

Books by Merline Lovelace

Silhouette Desire

Dreams and Schemes #872
†*Halloween Honeymoon* #1030
†*Wrong Bride, Right Groom* #1037
Undercover Groom #1220
§*Full Throttle* #1556
**Devlin and the Deep Blue Sea* #1726

Silhouette Intimate Moments

Somewhere in Time #593
**Night of the Jaguar* #637
**The Cowboy and the
    Cossack* #657
*Undercover Man #669
*Perfect Double #692
†*The 14th...and Forever* #764
Return to Sender #866
**If a Man Answers #878
*The Mercenary and the
    New Mom* #908
***A Man of His Word* #938
Mistaken Identity #987
***The Harder They Fall* #999
Special Report #1045
    "Final Approach...to Forever"
The Spy Who Loved Him #1052
***Twice in a Lifetime* #1071
*Hot as Ice #1129
*Texas Hero #1165
*To Love a Thief #1225
§*A Question of Intent* #1255
§*The Right Stuff* #1279
**Diamonds Can Be Deadly* #1411

Silhouette Books

Fortune's Children
Beauty and the Bodyguard

†*Holiday Honeymoons:
    Two Tickets to Paradise*
"His First Father's Day"

The Heart's Command
"Undercover Operations"

In Love and War
"A Military Affair"

**Code Name: Danger*
†*Holiday Honeymoons*
**Men of the Bar H
††*Destiny's Women*
§*To Protect and Defend*

MERLINE LOVELACE

spent twenty-three years in the Air Force, pulling tours in Vietnam, at the Pentagon and at bases all over the world. When she hung up her uniform, she decided to try her hand at writing. She's since had more than fifty novels published, with over seven million copies of her work in print. Watch for the next book in the Code Name: Danger series, *I'll Walk Alone,* coming from Silhouette Intimate Moments.

For the Old Farts gang—thanks for a fun day of war stories and tall tales about life on the patch!

Prologue

"You sleazy bucket of slime!"

Fury seared Elizabeth Moore's veins as she glared at the e-mail she'd printed out less than a half hour ago. In the light of the fat, round Baja moon she could just make out the message her fiancé had zinged her.

Correction.

Ex-fiancé.

Fuming, Liz ripped the e-mail into halves, then quarters, then jagged eighths. Waves, tinted to liquid gold by the moon, lapped at her bare ankles. With May slipping fast toward June, the heat of the Mexican night wrapped around her like a spongy blanket.

Digging her toes into the wet sand, Liz tore the eighths into sixteenths and threw them into the sea.

A receding wave carried off the scraps. The soggy bits floated for a few seconds before slowly sinking, drowning Liz's shattered dreams down with them.

"I can't believe I fell for such a jerk!"

The truth was only now beginning to register. The man she thought she'd share her life with, the fiancé who'd convinced her to take this job in Mexico while he racked up hours flying as a civilian contract pilot in Singapore had just zapped her an e-mail informing her he'd fallen for another woman. A Malay correspondent for NBC news by the name of Bambang Chawdar.

Bambang, for God's sake!

As if that wasn't bad enough, the bastard had also cleaned out their joint bank account.

Liz couldn't decide which infuriated her more—the fact that she'd convinced herself she was really in love with Donny Carter or that she'd remained faithful to him during their long separation.

"Seven months," she ground out. "Seven months I've lived like a damned nun."

She'd certainly had plenty of opportunities for sin. The oil crews she choppered to the offshore rig some forty miles off the Baja peninsula generally consisted of prime specimens. And when they came off their month-long rotations, they were hungry for female companionship. In the past seven months Liz had become an expert at dodging propositions from horny roughnecks and roustabouts. Most had required only a breezy smile or a firm "no, thanks." One or two had required a little more forceful response.

Liz certainly didn't feel like smiling now. She felt like hitting something. Or releasing her fury in a way that would soothe her battered pride *and* her pent-up frustration.

"I swear to God I'm going to jump the next half-way-sober male I meet!"

Her fierce vow carried clearly over the murmur of the Pacific. So did the amused drawl that came out of the darkness behind her.

"I'm sober, darlin'. And if you're looking for someone to jump, I'd be happy to oblige."

Liz's heart leapfrogged into her throat. She spun around, searching the dunes, until a dim shadow materialized. The moon was behind him. She couldn't make out his features, but the rest of him telegraphed a clear message. With each step he took toward her, a marquee inside her head flashed the words tall, rangy and buff.

What the heck was he doing out here on this isolated stretch of beach so late at night?

What was *she* doing here, alone and weaponless?

Cursing the anger that had made her leave both her cell phone and her collapsible baton in the Jeep parked up by the road, Liz stood her ground. She'd spent four years as an air force pilot. Her survival, evasion, resistance and escape trainers had taught her some pretty brutal moves. She could take this guy down if she needed to, despite his height and the impressive set of muscles she could just make out under his black T-shirt and jeans.

"I appreciate the offer," she replied with a lift of her chin, "but you might want to rethink it. The mood I'm in, a midnight tussle in the sand might not be a particularly enjoyable experience for you."

She saw his head angle, felt the prickly heat of his gaze as it traveled from her face to her stretchy white T-shirt to her cutoffs and the bare legs below. His face was a blur in the darkness, but she couldn't miss the wolfish grin that appeared as he stepped closer.

"I'll take my chances."

The slow drawl pegged him as an American. The laughter lacing it stirred an unexpected response from Liz. For an insane moment she was actually tempted to follow through with her rash vow. God knew she could use a little stud service, and this six-foot-plus hunk of hard muscle certainly looked like he could provide it.

Maybe it was the moon, she thought wildly. It had to be the moon exerting some weird gravitational pull, like the riptides so prevalent along the Baja coast. Whatever is was, Liz felt the surge of something dangerous. Powerful.

Caution shouted at her to step back, put a safe distance between her and this broad-shouldered stranger. Anger, singed pride and an uncharacteristic recklessness kept her in place as he moved closer.

She could see his features more clearly now. With the precision of an aviator verifying her course headings, she cataloged each one. Strong, square chin.

Nose with a slightly flattened bridge, as if it had taken a punch or two. White squint lines at the corners of his eyes. A grin that was pure sex.

"How about we…?"

A sharp crack split the night. Another followed a heartbeat later. The stranger spit out a curse, lunged forward, and slammed into Liz. She went down hard and landed on her butt in the shallow surf.

He went down with her, but rolled to his feet a second later and sprinted in the direction of the shots.

"Stay here!"

Like she could move? She was sprawled like a beached porpoise, wheezing from the impact of what had felt like 180 pounds of solid male.

It took Liz several seconds of painful effort to suck air back into her lungs before she, too, was up and running.

One

In the silent hours before dawn, only the occasional set of headlights stabbed through D.C.'s embassy district. The brick town houses lining a side street just off Massachusetts Avenue were shuttered and dark. From the outside, the elegant, three-story town house halfway down the block appeared as somnolent as its neighbors.

Light from a nearby streetlamp glowed dully on the discreet brass plaque mounted beside the front door. The plaque identified the building as housing the offices of the president's special envoy. Old-time Washingtonians knew the title was meaningless, one of dozens doled out after every election to wealthy campaign contributors itching to be part of the hustle and bustle of the capital. Only a handful of insiders knew the special envoy also doubled as the director of OMEGA, a secret agency that reported directly to the president and was activated as a last resort, when all other measures failed.

One of OMEGA's operatives was in the field now, and behind the darkened windows of the town house's third floor a high-tech operations center vibrated with rigidly restrained tension. The agent's controller sat at an elaborate console, his face tight with concentration.

"I didn't copy that last transmission, Rigger. Come again, please."

Joe Devlin, code name Rigger, responded with a heavy dose of disgust. "I said this part of the op just blew all to hell. I've got a corpse floating in the surf and I'm following a set of tracks fast getting washed away."

"Is the corpse our informant?"

"Negative. The contact said to look for someone in a Mazatland *Tigres* football jersey. The dead guy's in a Tommy Hilfiger T-shirt. My guess is he followed our pigeon, spooked him and got drilled in the process."

Everyone in the control center shared the frustration in Devlin's terse reply. Their first real lead— their *only* lead so far—to the ring suspected of murdering U.S. citizens and selling their identities to dangerous undesirables was now on the run.

Devlin's controller flicked a glance at the man listening to the exchange from a few yards away. Nick Jensen, code name Lightning, stood with the jacket of his Armani tux shoved back and his hands buried in the pockets of the hand-tailored trousers. He'd swung by the control center on his way home from one of the endless ceremonial dinners he regularly attended, and stayed for Rigger's anticipated report.

His wife, Mackenzie, sat perched on the edge of the console, sleek and elegant in a sheath of black silk and matching spike heels. With or without those three-inch stilettos, Mackenzie Blair Jensen was a force to be reckoned with. Formerly OMEGA's chief of communications, she now directed a team that supplied several agencies, including OMEGA, with equipment that would give any techie wet dreams. She remained as quiet as the others in the control center until Devlin came back on, huffing a little.

"Dammit! The shooter just jumped into a vehicle and took off. He's heading south on the coast road. Get some surveillance in the air ASAP."

"Will do. And I'll—" The controller broke off, eyeing a blinking red light. "Stand by, Rigger. I'm getting a flash override."

He switched frequencies, listened for a few seconds and switched back.

"We just intercepted a phone call to the Piedras Rojas police. There's a female on the line, reporting a shooting at approximately your location. Our listener says she sounds like an American."

"Well, hell! The blonde!"

"Come again?"

"There was a woman on the beach. I was just about to get rid of her when the bullets started flying."

Frowning, Lightning stepped forward. "What was

she doing at the rendezvous point so late at night? Acting as a lookout? A decoy?"

Three thousand miles away, Joe Devlin scrubbed a hand across the back of his neck. He'd spent almost six years as an OMEGA operative and had learned long ago never to take anyone at face value. He'd also learned to trust his instincts. The little he'd over-heard suggested the blonde had come out to the beach to conduct a personal exorcism.

"I don't think she's part of this op. Sounded like she just got a 'Dear Jane' letter and was working off steam."

Judging by her crack about living like a nun, it also sounded as though she'd built up a bad case of the hungries. Wishing like hell he'd had time to satisfy them, Devlin got back to business.

"We need to run her through the system and see what pops."

"Did you get a name?" Lightning asked.

"No, but I did tag her Jeep when she drove up."

Luckily, he'd arrived at the rendezvous site early. He'd seen the woman drive up and had tracked her from her Jeep to the water's edge. He'd planned to call in her tag and have OMEGA check her out, but matters had moved too fast. Drawing the numbers from his memory bank, Devlin relayed them along with a brief physical description.

"I'd say she's about twenty-eight or -nine. Five-six or so. Maybe 120 pounds. It was too dark to be sure, but I'm guessing her eyes were brown."

"We'll run her," Lightning advised. "How about the corpse? Did you find anything on him that gave you a clue as to his identity or why he showed up at your rendezvous?"

"I didn't have time to check. I'll go back now and do a search."

"Better do it quick. The locals will arrive on the scene shortly."

Devlin flipped the lid on what looked like an ordinary cell phone. Despite its innocuous appearance, the device contained enough ultrasonic signals, secure satellite frequencies and encryption capabilities to orchestrate an intergalactic expedition. Mackenzie Blair, bless her state-of-the-art soul, believed an operative couldn't carry too much in the way of communications into the field.

Keeping an eye out for the blonde, Devlin jogged back to the dark hump in the surf-washed sand. Damn! Whoever this guy was, his untimely demise sure put a kink in the mission.

Dropping to one knee, Devlin dragged out the tail of his T-shirt to use as a glove. A quick search turned up a fat wad of pesos wrapped with a rubber band, the kind of switchblade you could buy in any Mexican market and a container of dental floss.

Flipping the cell phone up again, Devlin punched a single key. "Robbery obviously wasn't the motive. The guy's still carrying his stash."

"Any ID?"

"Negative."

Lightning greeted that news with a grunt. "What about the woman? Can she ID you to the police?"

"Not by name, but she can give them a general description."

"Then I suggest you disappear. We'll track the locals' investigation. In the meantime you need to maintain your cover."

Devlin acknowledged the order but threw a regretful glance along the shoreline. He hated to leave with so many unanswered questions. Not to mention a very curvy, very delectable female who sounded as though she was in dire need of male companionship.

So long, Blondie. Sorry to leave you with this mess.

An hour later Liz wished fervently she'd hightailed it back to town instead of calling the local gendarmes. They were hardly CSI types.

The first officer on the scene had poked at the body with the toe of his boot, tugged on plastic gloves and shooed away the crabs. After feeling around in the victim's pockets, he extracted some objects and entered a sort of inventory in a notebook before ambling over to Liz.

She told him what happened. He made a few more notes and asked her if she knew the deceased. She didn't.

About that time, Subcommandante Carlos Rivera and the crime scene unit arrived. Liz waited while the inspector studied the corpse and conferred with the uniformed officer. Finally he turned his attention to her. Slowly and methodically, he went over every word of her statement. Such as it was.

"You say you do not know the identity of the man who has been shot?"

"No, I don't."

"What about this Americano? The one you say appeared out of the darkness?"

"I don't know his identity, either."

"Yet you spoke with him."

Liz had done more than speak with the guy. She'd responded to the laughter in his voice and that damned grin and let the man get close enough to touch her. Worse, she'd *wanted* him to touch her. Okay, more than touch her. She'd actually entertained notions of rolling around in the surf with him. How stupid was that?

Too stupid to admit to Subcommandante Rivera.

"We only exchanged a few words," she muttered.

The inspector nodded, his face grave beneath the visor of his cap. "Perhaps you will be so kind as to explain again what brought you to such an isolated spot at this late hour."

Liz dragged a hand through her cropped hair. She'd gone through this with the first officer on the scene. It didn't sound any better the second time around.

"I received news that upset me. I needed to vent."

"And you could not do this in Piedras Rojas, where you live?"

After receiving Donny's e-mail, Liz had thought about stopping by her favorite cantina in town and drinking herself into a stupor. But she had a flight tomorrow morning. Her training and professionalism went too deep to climb into a cockpit hung over. Since the small, sleepy village of Piedras Rojas offered no other outlet for her anger, she'd headed for the beach some miles south of town.

Piedras rojas. Red stones. When the sun sank toward the sea and set the cliffs along this stretch of coast aflame, there wasn't a more awesome sight anywhere in the world. The other twenty-three and a half hours of the day, dust swirled, trees drooped, and the locals baked in the unrelenting heat.

For all these months Liz had ignored the dust and the heat and the flies and socked away every peso she earned ferrying crews out to and back from the offshore drill site. She and Donny had talked about purchasing a fleet of helos and starting their own charter service. Anxious to make the dream a reality, Liz had used her savings as collateral and taken out a loan for deposit on their first bird. The sleek little Sikorsky single-pilot craft had a Rolls Royce turbine engine, a 2,000-pound load capacity and the best auto-rotational characteristics of any helicopter flying today.

Now her savings were gone, she'd have to forfeit the nonrefundable deposit and she still had to make good on the damned loan. Pissed all over again, Liz shoved her fists into the pockets of her cutoffs.

"No, I couldn't work off steam in town. Look,

Subcommandante, I've told you everything I know. Are we done here?"

"We are done. For now."

"Fine. I'll head back to town."

With a curt nod, she turned and plowed through the dunes. Talk about your all-around crappy nights! This one ranked right up there with the night she'd said goodbye to Donny. Liz had dreaded another long separation. He'd seemed eager to return to Malaysia and finish out his contract. Too eager, she now knew. He wanted to get back to Bambang.

Bambang. God!

Liz shoved her Jeep into gear, slinging mental arrows at her former fiancé. To her surprise, she had trouble putting a face on the target. The tall, lanky American who'd appeared out of the night seemed to have crowded Donny out of her head. No wonder! The man had shaved a good five years off her life popping up like that.

If and when she met up with him again, Mr. No-Name would have to answer a few pointed questions. Like why he'd been out here at the beach so late at night. And why he'd disappeared. And whether he knew who had put a bullet into the dead man's skull.

As Liz navigated the narrow road that led up from the beach and along the rocky cliffs, the questions buzzed around inside her head like pesky flies.

They were still buzzing the next morning when she pulled into the small regional airport that serviced the resorts springing up along this stretch of the Mexican Riviera.

The temperature was already climbing toward the predicted high of one hundred plus. Liz threw a glance at the wind sock drooping in the heat above the building that served as both terminal and tower and knew she'd be swimming inside her flight suit by the time she returned from her run. Sighing, she retrieved her flyaway bag from the passenger seat.

The corrugated tin Quonset hut that constituted Aero Baja's hangar and operations center occupied a patch of rock- and cactus-studded red dirt to the left of the terminal. Liz was one of three Aero Baja helicopter pilots under contract to the American-Mexican Petroleum Company to ferry crews and supplies to the giant rig forty miles off the coast. All of the pilots were qualified in a variety of craft, but their platform here at Piedras Rojas was the Bell Ranger 412.

The Ranger sat on the red dirt pad, being prepped by Aero Baja's chief mechanic. This particular model had been configured for over-water operations by a single pilot, could carry up to fourteen passengers and cruised at 120 knots. The aircraft was almost as old as Liz. Thankfully, it had been updated with two GPS receivers, a new altimeter and a marine band radio in addition to the usual UHF, VHF and HF radios. It looked and handled like a mosquito on a leash after the heavily armed, superpowered choppers Liz had flown in the air force, but she'd gotten used to its aerodynamics and thoroughly enjoyed taking it up.

The mechanic prepping the Ranger had seen as much service as the aircraft itself. Retired after thirty-plus years with the Mexican air force, Jorge Garcia could take the Ranger apart and put it back together in his sleep.

Liz had formed a close friendship with the affable, mustachioed mechanic during her months in Mexico. She couldn't count the number of beers they'd shared after work or the meals his wife, Maria, had fed her. Hefting her flight bag, Liz joined him on the pad.

"*Buenos días,* Jorge."

"*Buenos días,* Lizetta."

His pet name for her usually produced a smile. Liz had to work to dredge one up this morning. She was gritty-eyed after the late-night session on the beach and still steaming over Donny's betrayal.

"Is the Ranger ready to fly?"

Grinning, Jorge patted the helicopter's fuselage with a callused palm. "She is."

Stowing her bag in the cockpit, Liz did a careful walk-around. The American-Mexican Petroleum Company was paying her serious bucks to ferry its cargo and crews. She took her responsibilities to AmMex and to her passengers seriously. Before transporting anything or anyone out to the patch, as they referred to the monster rising up out of the sea, she made sure her craft was airworthy.

Jorge followed, marking off the checklist items as

Liz completed them. They had worked their way from the rear rotor to the main-engine driveshaft before Liz dropped a casual question.

"Did you hear any rumors about some trouble last night?"

There hadn't been any mention of a shooting in Piedras Rojas' morning newspaper. Probably because Piedras Rojas didn't have a newspaper, morning or otherwise.

"What kind of trouble?"

"Gunshots down at the beach just after midnight. A dead body, maybe."

The mechanic's eyes rounded above his bushy black mustache. "Are you saying you go to the beach after midnight?

"Yes."

"Alone?"

"It started out that way."

"Ayyyy, Lizetta, that is not wise!"

She certainly couldn't argue the point. Last night's misadventure had driven home just how *unwise.*

Despite its slow pace and *mañana* approach to just about everything, Piedras Rojas was only a half-hour drive from La Paz, situated at the very tip of the Baja California peninsula. The city had become a major crime center since antidrug operations in the Caribbean had forced Colombian drug lords to shift their operations to the Pacific coast.

The cartels' vehicle of choice for their smuggling trade was the Mexican tuna fleet that operated out of ports all along the coast. The tuna boats were fast, long-range clippers that could spend months at sea. In a good year the fleet generated approximately a hundred million dollars in tuna revenue. A single boat could carry a load of cocaine worth twice that. As a result, drugs, corruption and violence had become a part of life in this corner of the world.

"Then why do you go to the beach so late?" Jorge wanted to know.

"Donny sent me an e-mail." The words tasted as sour as three-day-old frijoles. "He's dumped me. Seems he's fallen for a foreign news correspondent."

The mechanic fired off a string of highly colorful Spanish. Liz caught only a few of the more exotic phrases, but they were enough to produce a reluctant smile.

"That was pretty much my reaction, too."

Spitting out a final curse, Jorge squinted at her through the iridescent waves of heat rising from the dirt pad.

"Will you go back to the States now?"

"Maybe. I haven't decided."

"But the helo you have saved every peso to buy! The charter service you plan to start! You do not need this pig, this Donny. You can start your own company without him."

Liz didn't tell him about her now-empty bank account. No sense broadcasting her monumental stupidity in making Donny joint on her account when he'd somehow never got around to putting her on his.

Nor did she care to reveal that she didn't have enough cash left to cover her rent, due tomorrow. She'd have to swallow her pride and ask the smarmy AmMex on-site rep for an advance on next month's salary. Trying not to wince at the prospect, Liz repeated her often made promise.

"When I do open my own charter service, you will most definitely be my chief mechanic."

"*Bueno!* We make a good team, yes?"

"That we do."

Satisfied, Jorge returned his attention to the pre-flight checklist. While he inspected the main driveshaft forward coupling for grease leakage, Liz checked the engine inlet and plenum to make sure they were clear of obstructions. The rumble of an approaching vehicle announced the arrival of their passengers.

The bus pulled up at the terminal and a half-dozen men filed into the building. Liz went back to the pre-flight inspection, knowing it would take the sleepy-eyed terminal official a good half hour to search the crew members' bags for drugs and alcohol, weigh both men and luggage and show them a video explaining the safe boarding and ditching of a heli-copter at sea. The video would play twice, once in English, once in Spanish. Hopefully, the non-English-, non-Spanish-speaking crewmen would get the idea from the video.

When the crew filed out of the terminal, Liz pasted on a smile and went to double-check their IDs against the manifest provided by AmMex. Like most of the men working the big rigs, these were a mixed bag of nationalities and skills.

A big, beefy Irish driller led the pack. A Filipino welder followed, then a Mexican radio operator and two Venezuelan cooks. When the last passenger stepped forward, Liz read off his name from the manifest.

"Devlin, Joe."

"Yes, ma'am."

The slow drawl brought her head whipping up. "It's you!"

He responded to that with the same wolfish grin he'd given her last night. "Yes, ma'am."

Two

Devlin waited while a variety of expressions flickered across the face of the woman OMEGA had ID'd as Elizabeth Moore. He'd spent most of what was left of the night after the fiasco on the beach assimilating the background data headquarters had assembled on her.

He had to admit the info was pretty impressive. After completing USAF flight school at the top of her class, Moore had opted to fly rotary wing aircraft because that's what her father had flown during his long and distinguished military career. Brigadier General Moore had died of a massive coronary less than a year after his daughter pinned on her wings, but she'd lived up to both his name and his reputation as a crack pilot. She'd spent four years inserting special-ops teams into particularly nasty spots all over the globe before leaving the military with the announced intention of opening her own charter service.

Unfortunately for her, Captain Moore's smarts didn't extend to her choice in men. According to OMEGA's hastily assembled dossier, she'd fallen for a jerk by the name of Donald Carter and let him talk her into taking this boring, if highly lucrative, job as a contract pilot in Mexico while he did his thing in Malaysia. In recent months said jerk had reportedly been getting his rocks off with a Malaysian newswoman.

It didn't take a NASA engineer to fit the pieces together. Obviously, Moore had just found out about her fiancé's affair. Just as obviously, she'd gone to the beach last night determined to flush the bastard out of her system.

Devlin wished to hell he'd been able to help with the flushing. The woman looked even better in the bright light of day than she had in the glow of the moon, and she'd looked damned good then! Her zippered flight suit didn't display her long, sexy legs the way her cutoffs had, but the tan fabric hugged her curves very nicely. Very nicely indeed. Devlin almost hated to depart for the oil rig.

Assuming he did depart. The issue looked doubtful at the moment, judging by the suspicion in Moore's brown eyes.

"Jorge!" Her face tight, she called to a mechanic

in grease-stained overalls. "Get our passengers briefed and strapped in. Devlin, you come with me."

She shoved the clipboard at the crew chief and stalked toward the corrugated tin hangar. Devlin followed, eyeing her trim behind with real appreciation.

"In here."

She led the way into an office with a beat-up metal desk, a single file cabinet and an ancient air conditioner rattling in the window. The walls were decorated with the usual clutter seen in operations shacks around the world. Weather updates. Flight schedules. Area NOTAMs. A fly-specked calendar depicting a luscious Miss May falling out of a blouse unbuttoned almost to her navel.

Devlin spared Miss May only a passing glance. Ms. Moore held his full attention. Her blunt-cut hair swirled in a silky arc as she slammed the door behind them and spun around.

The woman didn't waste time. Spearing him with a narrow-eyed stare, she launched a direct attack. "What were you doing on the beach last night?"

Devlin had anticipated this meeting since learning Moore's identity and had his cover ready. Luckily, it fit him like a second skin. Born and raised amid the oil fields of Oklahoma, he'd worked his way up from mud man to pipe handler to site supervisor. Along the way he'd accumulated undergraduate and graduate degrees in petroleum engineering and drilled holes in every ocean floor from the Gulf of Aden to the Bering Strait.

He'd also racked up a brief marriage and quick divorce. Candace had insisted his pay and benefits compensated for the long separations, but had soon gone looking for other distractions. Devlin didn't blame her. Divorce was an occupational hazard in his line of work.

His life had become even more erratic after he'd joined the OMEGA team. Nick Jensen, aka Lightning, had recruited him just months after terrorists blew up an American-operated rig in international waters off the coast of Kuwait. Devlin had lost friends in that explosion and had jumped at the chance to use his civilian cover as a means of bringing the murdering bastards to justice.

Now another friend had disappeared. A close friend. And a real badass who specialized in transporting underage aliens across the border to sell into sexual slavery had been picked up while using Harry Johnson's passport and ID. Law enforcement officials from a dozen different agencies had grilled the imposter but didn't get much. Turned out he'd never met the man who'd supplied the stolen documents. They'd been left at a designated drop site after the recipient had deposited a hefty sum in the same location.

Nor had Harry's body ever been recovered. All his fiancée knew, all anyone knew, was that Harry had disappeared after rotating off an AmMex oil rig, and someone using his passport had popped up on U.S. customs screens a few weeks later. What little intelligence OMEGA had been able to gather indicated the brains behind the ring supplying stolen passports operated out of this general vicinity. Devlin fully intended to nail the bastard. He wouldn't let anyone— Captain Moore included—jeopardize this mission.

Hitching a hip on the desk, he responded to her sharp question with a deliberate combination of fact and fiction. "I went to the beach last night to meet someone."

That part was true. What came next wasn't.

"He said he had a one-time good deal for me on personal gear for use on the rig."

"Why didn't he come to your hotel in to conduct this sale?"

"My guess is he lifted the equipment from a roust-about, either on the rig or after he came off."

That didn't happen often, but it did happen. Rig crews hailed from just about every country on the planet. That made communication a distinct challenge. Their staggered rotations also presented opportunities for high-dollar tools and unsecured personal items to disappear.

Still suspicious, Moore tapped a booted toe. "So who fired the shots? This light-fingered entrepreneur?"

"Maybe. Or maybe the man he stole from. The shooter had departed the scene when I reached his victim."

"This victim. Was he dead when you got to him?"

"He took a bullet between the eyes. You don't get much deader than that."

Her foot tapped the floor again. Once. Twice.

"You didn't kill him," she said, scowling. "I could have vouched for that. So why did you disappear?"

"I only arrived in Mexico with the replacement crew yesterday." Another lie, followed by another truth. "But I've been around enough to know you don't get mixed up in an incident like this unless you want to spend some not-so-quality time with the *federales*."

"So you left me to do the explaining?"

The disdain in her eyes stung. Devlin deflected it with a shrug. "I went back to look for you. You had departed the scene, too."

"Wrong! I ran up to my car to get my cell phone and call the police."

He hooked an incredulous brow. "And you hung around to wait for them?"

"Someone had to."

He let that pointed barb hang on the air for a moment before giving her a smile of genuine regret. "I have to admit, I had to think twice about leaving. If I'd stuck around, I might have gotten real lucky."

The ploy worked. The reminder of her rash vow brought her chin up and a flush to her cheeks.

"Not hardly, Devlin. You're not my type."

"Best I recall, you didn't specify a type last night."

The pink in her cheeks deepened to brick. "Yeah, well, that was last night."

He pushed off the desk and moved closer. She wasn't wearing a speck of makeup that he could see, but her gold-flecked brown eyes didn't need any goopy mascara to emphasize either their depth or their intelligence. And he had to admit the light dusting of freckles across her nose turned him on. That, and her unique scent. It drifted on an air-conditioned breeze, a tantalizing combination of soap and perspiration and aviation fuel.

He needed to keep her off balance, he reminded himself. Prevent her from probing too deeply. Throwing himself into the task, he gave her a wicked grin.

"How about this morning? Nothing says we can't take up where we left off."

"Oh, sure! With a rotation crew waiting outside in the heat?"

"I'm game if you are."

Liz shook her head, suspended between suspicion and disbelief. "You're something else, cowboy."

"Yes, ma'am. I do believe I've been told that once or twice."

She was damned if she could figure this guy out. He certainly looked like the roustabout he claimed to be. The sun had bleached his close-cut hair to golden brown. The white squint lines she'd noticed last night cut into skin tanned to dark oak by wind and sun. A couple days' stubble darkened his cheeks and chin, as if he was getting a head start on the bushy beard most of the crews sprouted while on the rig. Then there was the palm he slid under her hair to circle her nape. It was callused and leather tough.

Liz stiffened at the touch of his skin against hers.

Her eyes met his and telegraphed an unmistakable warning, which he ignored.

"If we can't finish what we started," he murmured, his gaze sliding downward to fix on her mouth, "how about we just settle for a kiss?"

Holding her in place with that thorny palm, he bent and brushed her lips with his.

Liz stood stiff, debating whether to whip up a knee or ream out his gut with her elbow. Devlin took full advantage of the hesitation, as brief as it was. Shifting his stance, he brought his mouth came down on hers with a hunger Liz hadn't tasted in seven months.

Or longer, she realized with a jolt as his lips molded hers. To her chagrin, she couldn't *remember* the last time a man had kissed her as if he meant it. Donny's affectionate pecks hadn't come close to packing this powerful a charge.

She savored the sizzle for a moment, maybe two, before breaking the contact. Feeling the loss of warmth immediately, she buried it in biting sarcasm.

"Finished flexing your masculinity, cowboy?"

"Guess so."

"Then I'll chalk this little interlude up to my stupid remark last night and let you walk out of here." She looked him square in the eye. "Touch me again without my permission, however, and you'll be drilling for something besides Mexican crude."

Spinning on her heel, she strode out into the smothering heat. Jorge was waiting beside the pad with a question in his eyes. Liz answered it with a small shake of her head and brisk order tossed over her shoulder to the man who'd followed her from the operations shack.

"Get aboard and buckle up."

Devlin joined his companions in the passenger compartment. Only after Liz had climbed into the cockpit and buckled her seat harness did she realize she'd bought his story about the supposed thief he'd gone to meet last night.

Frowning, she strapped on her kneeboard and forced herself to concentrate on the power-up sequence checklist. The engines whined. The forty-four feet of main rotor blades churned up dust, slowly at first, then in a reddish whirlwind. The aircraft began to shimmy as Liz radioed the tower.

Once she received clearance to taxi, her years of training and experience kicked in. Flying an aircraft that operated in both horizontal and vertical planes required a level of coordination not all pilots possessed. As always, getting her bird in the air and shifting smoothly from one plane to the other produced an adrenaline rush.

Her second in less than twenty minutes, Liz thought as she banked and aimed for the blue, sparkling Pacific. Her mouth still tingled from the kiss Devlin had laid on her.

Scowling behind her mirrored sunglasses, she set a course for floating the platform designated American-Mexican Petroleum Company Drill Site 237.

* * *

She must have made the run to AM-237 forty or fifty times in the past seven months. Every time, the sheer immensity of the ultradeepwater semisubmersible rig inspired awe. It was as big as a city block—a floating platform spiked by two giant cranes and a derrick that rose to impossible heights.

Anchored to the ocean floor by chains and 45,000-pound anchors, the superstructure sat on massive pontoons and four corner columns. Once the platform was positioned over a drill site, the columns were flooded with seawater. This caused the pontoons to sink to a predetermined depth and lessened the platform's surface movement, making it relatively stable.

Relative being the key word. To a pilot aiming for the helideck that jutted out over the rig's bow some seven stories above the water, even slight up and down movement had to be taken into consideration. The trick was to contact the helideck at its highest point and ride it down. Slamming into it on the way up stressed the landing gear and made the passengers just a tad nervous.

Liz chose a leeward approach and put the helo into a descending spiral a quarter of a mile out. The fat orange flanges for pumping the crude into tankers stood out like beacons on the east side. She lined up on the flanges to begin her final approach.

"AM-237, this is Aero Baja 214 on final."

"Roger, 214. We have you on the scope. We're putting out the welcome mat."

While the rig's two crane operators lowered the booms to clear the airspace, a support ship maneuvered into position at the pontoon closest to the helideck. The ship's mission was to pick up survivors if the incoming aircraft hit the drink instead of the deck.

"The LO is standing by."

The rig's landing officer climbed onto the pad, clearly visible in his bright yellow vest.

"I see him," Liz acknowledged.

Although this was only a secondary duty for him, she knew he'd been doing it a long time and trusted him to guide her in. Keeping one eye on his arm signals and another on the instrument panel, she put her aircraft into a hover above the deck and brought her down.

The skids touched, lifted and settled with a small thump. While the red-vested tie-down crew ducked under the blades to anchor the helicopter to the deck, Liz powered down. Once the blades had chugged to a halt, she keyed her mike.

"Welcome to AM-237, gentlemen."

Swinging a leg over the stick, she clambered into the cargo compartment.

"Claim your gear and pass it to the deckhands," she instructed the new arrivals. "Make sure you hang on to the lifelines when you climb out onto the pad."

The old-timers knew the drill, but there were questions in the eyes of a couple of obvious newcomers. Liz repeated the instructions in Spanish, then in elaborate pantomime. Looking both doubtful and nervous, the newbies poked their heads outside the hatch. Liz saw several Adam's apples bounce and knuckles turn white as the crewmen measured the distance from the pad to the ocean below.

"Don't piss yourself," the beefy Irishman advised one of the Venezuelans. "Just hang on to that strap. Out you go now, there's a good lad."

Since the brawny oilman supplemented his friendly words of encouragement with a solid thump between the shoulder blades, the cargo compartment soon emptied of everyone but Liz and Devlin. Passing his gear bag to a waiting deckhand, he turned back to her.

"How often do you make this run?"

"Five maybe six times a month. Depends on whether they need supplies or there's a crew rotating off."

"Maybe I'll see you on your next run."

"Maybe."

He took a step toward her, his sun-streaked hair ruffled by the wind whistling through the open hatch. "Do I have your permission?"

"My permission? For…? Oh! No, as a matter of fact, you don't. No touching, Devlin, and definitely no kissing."

"Sure you won't reconsider? It's going to be a long twenty-eight days out here."

"Just grin and bear it."

"I'll do my best."

Tipping her a two-fingered salute, he exited the aircraft and made his way to the stairs leading to the main deck.

Liz saw to the unloading of the replenishment supplies and accepted the sealed outgoing mail pouch, but instructed the landing officer to wait before bringing up the departing crew members.

"I need to talk to the company rep," she informed him, holding back her wind-whipped hair with one hand. "Do you know where he is?"

"Try the galley. Conrad is usually there this time of morning, swilling coffee and shooting off his… Er, shooting the breeze."

She gave the LO a wry smile. She'd dealt with AmMex Petroleum's on-site representative before. She had no doubt she would find him pontificating to anyone unfortunate enough to be stuck in his immediate vicinity.

She took the stairs, crossed the deck to the main superstructure and entered a world like none other. The ever-present reek of fresh paint and diesel fuel flavored the air. Machinery constantly in motion thumped out the rig's steady heartbeat. Metal creaked as the massive platform rode the waves.

The giant anchors and stabilizers minimized the motion until it was almost imperceptible, but Liz had to lay a palm against the bulkhead once or twice as she followed the scent of fried onions to the galley. Sure enough, the AmMex on-site rep was sprawled in a mess chair at the officers' table, holding forth.

Big and amiable and impervious to all attempts to shut him up, Conrad Wallace never seemed to tire of the sound of his own voice. Today's topic appeared to be a crew Ping-Pong tournament that evidently didn't come off to Wallace's satisfaction. The rig's Pakistani-born doctor sat across from him with a glazed expression on her face. When she spotted Liz, relief sprang into her eyes.

"Hello, Elizabeth. Did you bring the waterproof cast liners I ordered?"

"Sure did."

"What about the metronidazole tablets?"

"They're on back order, but marked priority. I'll fly them out as soon as they arrive."

"Thank you. I need them. Excuse me, Conrad. I must go inventory the new supplies."

She hurried out, leaving Liz to help herself to the coffee before joining Wallace at the gleaming teak table reserved for the rig's officers. The officers lived well out here on the patch, as did the hundred-plus crew members. Accommodations included hotel-class rooms, a galley that served international cuisine, a cinema showing satellite TV and movies and a gym that would get a gold stamp of approval from Arnold Schwarzenegger. Oil companies had to provide such facilities along with high-dollar salaries to induce men and women to live surrounded by miles of empty water for months at a time.

Cradling her coffee, Liz sank into a padded captain's chair. The company man shifted his bulk in her direction and picked up almost where he'd left off.

"We were talking about the fluke shot that won the

crew Ping-Pong tournament last night. Did anyone tell you about it?"

"No, I just got down."

"It was crazy. The ball ricocheted off a steam pipe, hit the forehead of one of the watchers and slammed back on the table. No way the referee should have allowed that shot, but you know how these foreigners are. They make up their own rules as they go."

Liz started to remind the man the rig sat in Mexican territorial waters and *he* was the foreigner here but didn't want to set him off on a new tangent. Instead, she cut straight to the point.

"I need an advance on next month's salary."

Wallace blinked at the abrupt change of topic and pursed his lips. Liz recognized his pinched expression. She categorized it as his company face.

"Payday was last week," he pontificated, as if she weren't well aware of that basic fact. "Don't tell me you've already run through the exorbitant flight pay AmMex shells out to you."

Her supposedly "exorbitant" flight pay was an old issue, one that came up every time Liz renewed her contract.

"What I did with my pay is my business, Conrad."

Frowning at the cool reply, Wallace shifted in his seat. He was a big man, but soft around the middle. Not lean and hard like the roughnecks who wrestled pipe or the roustabouts who performed general maintenance work.

Not like Joe Devlin.

Irritated at the way the man kept popping into her head, Liz laid out her requirement. "I need six hundred."

Living was considerably cheaper in Mexico than in the States, thank goodness. That amount would cover the payment due on the loan and get her though to the next payday with no problem.

"Six hundred?" Wallace echoed, looking as horrified as a man asked to sacrifice his firstborn child.

Liz should have known he'd balk. The man managed a multimillion-dollar operating budget, yet was so tight he squeaked when he walked.

"You know, Conrad, you're the perfect company man. You think every cent you dole out comes out of your own pocket."

"Well, it does! Anything that impacts the company's bottom line affects its profit margin, which in turn affects its stock value. Since I receive a large portion of my compensation and retirement in stock options, I'm obligated—"

"I know the spiel," Liz interrupted ruthlessly. It was the only way to get through to the man. "You're obligated to act as a responsible guardian of company funds. Are you going to give me the six hundred or not?"

"All right. All right. I will. But you'll have to sign a voucher. Let's go down to my office."

Liz lifted her bird off the patch a half hour later with a check for the six hundred zippered into her jumpsuit pocket and an exuberant crew strapped into the passenger compartment.

Ahead stretched forty minutes of open sea. Liz had flown the route so many times she could put her conscious mind on autopilot and switch her thoughts to the mess Donny had landed her in.

She thought briefly of hiring a lawyer and going after him. Pride and utter disgust at her own stupidity quashed that idea. She'd just have to tough it out down here in Mexico for a while longer. If she watched her pennies, she should be able to repay the loan she'd taken out for that blasted nonrefundable deposit and get back on her feet within a few months.

Which meant she'd probably ferry Devlin back to shore when he rotated off the patch.

Hell, there he was again! Bouncing around inside her head like a damned yo-yo. She couldn't seem to get him out. Or his outrageous offer of stud service.

What the heck. If Liz *did* ferry him back to shore a few weeks from now, maybe she should take him up on the offer. She didn't quite trust the man. And she wasn't sure she bought his story about last night's events. Yet she had to admit the kiss he'd laid on her this morning had curled her toes inside her boots.

Like a DVD played in digital high definition, she saw again the glint in Devlin's eyes as he bent toward her, felt the heat of his mouth on hers and cursed herself for being a fool.

Dumped less than ten hours ago by one man and

here she was, fantasizing about another! How many kinds of an idiot did that make her?

Thoroughly disgusted, Liz skimmed her bird toward the postcard-perfect shoreline.

The men poured out as soon as the skids touched down and Jorge set the chocks. Most clutched e-tickets and were eager to get through customs and onto the bus to La Paz. Once there, they'd board the jets that would carry them to homes scattered from the Azores to the Strait of Malacca. A few intended to head for town and the women who would soon relieve them of a healthy portion of their accumulated pay. First they had to be cleared by the Mexican official who routinely met Liz's incoming flight.

Today there were two officials. She recognized the bored-looking bureaucrat who usually rubber-stamped the crew's papers. The other she hadn't seen before.

"What's up?" she asked Jorge as she hefted the mail pouch from the empty copilot's seat. "Why the extra *funcionario?*

"I do not know."

Interesting. Maybe Devlin's story had basis in fact. Maybe a deckhand *had* stolen some valuable equipment and authorities were now shaking down all crews coming off the rig. Funny Wallace didn't mention the theft to her, though. The company rep was such a motormouth about everything else.

"Perhaps it has something to do with this," Jorge said.

He dragged a folded piece of paper from the pocket

of his overalls. It was a flier with a Xerox photo of a man Liz didn't recognize. Her eyes widened as she translated the Spanish under the picture.

"Does this say what I think it does?"

"¡*Sí!* There is a reward. Fifty thousand pesos for information about whoever shot this man last night."

"Last night, huh?"

Liz licked suddenly dry lips. The image of a body floating in the surf jumped into her head.

"This is Martín Alvarez," Jorge said grimly.

The name didn't register. Her expression must have indicated as much, as Jorge clicked his tongue like a hyperactive cricket.

"Ayyyyy, Lizetta! You do not know him?"

"No."

"He is the nephew of Eduardo Alvarez. The one known as El Tiburón."

El Tiburón. The Shark. *That* registered.

Goose bumps prickled Liz's skin. Gulping, she stared at the grainy photo of the nephew of one of the biggest, baddest members of the Mexican mafia.

Three

El Tiburón. The nickname echoed in Liz's head all day. She'd heard about the man from various sources during her months in Mexico, and what she'd heard was *not* good.

She drove home after work to peel off her sweat-soaked flight suit and to shower. Cool and comfortable in flip-flops, jeans and sleeveless cotton blouse, she got back in the Jeep and navigated the narrow streets to her favorite cantina for dinner. A few tourists wandered through the shops, but most had retreated to the luxury resorts strung along the cliffs for cocktails by the pool.

El Poco Lobo was crowded with shop owners, street vendors and boatmen back from fishing charters and swim or snorkeling tours. The locals jammed elbow to elbow at the smoky bar. Empty Corona bottles filled with red pebbles formed a pyramid against the flyspecked mirror backing the bar. Liz usually ate at one of the rickety tables outside, but the cantina owner waved her inside.

"Hola, Elizabeth."

"Hola, Anita."

Avid interest filled the woman's black eyes. "Is it true what we hear? You were at the beach last night?"

"Yes. What's the special this evening?"

"Beans and roast pork. I will get you a dish and you will tell us what happens, yes?"

Hunching over her heaping plate of succulent *carne asada*, Liz did her best to play down her role in the night's events. Yes, she'd heard the shots, she said in a reprise of her conversation with Subcommandante Rivera. No, she didn't see who fired them. And no, she didn't know who'd been shot until Jorge told her this morning.

She managed to dodge most of the more persistent of her questioners. Unfortunately, she couldn't dodge the two men who were waiting for her when she parked her Jeep in its usual place under the droopy jacaranda tree that shaded the stairs to her apartment.

The two tough-looking strangers stepped from behind the massive, twisted trunk. One was short and squat and walked with a limp. The other wore a lavender shirt, pleated black slacks and black-and-white wingtip shoes. The wingtips were bad enough. The shoulder holster he didn't bother to conceal was worse.

"El Tiburón wishes to speak with you," the shorter of the two said in English.

"What if I don't wish to speak with El Tiburón?"

The men obviously considered the question rhetorical, as neither bothered to answer. Nor did they seem particularly worried about the hand she'd slipped into the side pocket of the driver's door. She discovered why when Wingtips produced the collapsible baton she usually kept there.

"Is this what you search for?"

With a small smile, he passed her the baton and folded himself into the Jeep's cramped backseat. Short Guy settled in the front passenger seat.

"Take the coast road south, toward Cabo San Lucas. We will tell you where to turn off."

Liz weighed her options. She could refuse to comply but suspected that might result in something unpleasant. Like a gun barrel whacked up alongside her head. She could try shouting for help while wielding the baton, which would no doubt result in similar consequences. Or she could go along for the ride.

Shrugging, she rekeyed the ignition and backed out from under the tree. As she negotiated the narrow space, she regretted swinging by her apartment to change after work. Flip-flops and jeans weren't exactly what she would have chosen to wear for a meeting with the local mafia king. Not that the flight suit would have provided much more protection against an Uzi. Wishing fervently for a bulletproof vest, Liz took the coast road toward Cabo.

The Pacific sparkled on her left. To her right, cactus speared out of the sunbaked Baja desert. As they neared the tip of the peninsula, the cliffs lining the shore grew more rugged and the resorts more opulent. Some kilometers past Todos Santos, Short Guy directed her to turn onto a gravel road. This led to a high-walled adobe fence. Broken glass shards in a variety of greens and browns provided a jagged barrier atop the adobe. Rolled concertina wire added another welcoming touch to the vicious glass.

Liz slowed before an elaborately carved iron gate. Her escort waved to the armed guards manning the thatch-roofed shack at the entrance. When they obligingly hit the switch, the gates swung open to reveal an avenue of tall, swaying palms. They shut behind the Jeep with a clank that resounded in Liz's ears like a clap of doom.

Wrapping her sweaty palms around the wheel, she followed the drive through the kind of tropical paradise usually seen only at five-star resorts. Lush green grass was manicured to within an inch of its life. Bushes exploded with red and pink and orange bougainvillea. Fountains splashed at regular intervals.

At the end of the drive sat a sprawling adobe structure constructed from the native ochre-colored mud. The wood trim at the windows and doors was painted almost the same shade of turquoise as the Sea of Cortez on a sunny day. Escorted by Short Guy and

Wingtips, Liz exited the Jeep and stepped out of the blazing sun into a blessedly cool foyer.

"This way."

Her flip-flops slapped against beautifully glazed marble tiles as she passed through a succession of open, airy rooms before being ushered into what could have passed for a Wall Street executive's office. Stock quotes flashed across the plasma TV screen hung on one wall. A state-of-the art pedestal computer with a twenty-three-inch monitor sat on the massive slab of glass that served as a desk. The only personal touch was what looked like a family photo in a silver frame.

The snapshot had been taken aboard a gleaming white yacht. A trim, athletic-looking man in swimming trunks lounged in a deck chair. He looked relaxed and happy, an arm hooked around the shoulders of the woman lounging next to him. She laughed up at him while two children—kids? grandkids?—stood behind them and mugged for the camera.

The woman was draped in enough jewelry to open her own branch of Tiffany's. A rock the size of Rhode Island sparkled on her ring finger. The diamond studs in her ears had to have weighed two carats each. Her gold Rolex was studded with sapphires.

The man beside her wore only a gold chain with some kind of charm hooked through it. The pale, triangular object nestled against his dark chest hair. It was a shark's tooth, Liz realized with a gulp. From what had to be one hell of a fish. Scenes from the movie *Jaws* were flashing through her head when a side door opened.

The man who entered was the same one in the photo. Tall and trim, with neatly cut salt-and-pepper hair, he wore tan slacks and a short-sleeved white shirt with an embroidered monogram on the breast pocket.

"Welcome to my home, Ms. Moore."

He held out his hand. Liz offered hers more slowly. He didn't *look* as though he intended to chop it off. Then again, The Shark had a reputation for devouring his enemies whole.

"Thank you for agreeing to speak with me."

"Did I have a choice?"

"One always has a choice. Please, be seated."

He waved her to one of the leather chairs grouped around a glass coffee table and took the other.

"Would you care for a drink after your long drive? We have Dos Equis on ice. I believe that is the brand you prefer."

Uh-oh. This guy knew her preference in beer. A shiver slithered down Liz's spine as she wondered what else he knew about her.

A bunch, she learned after she politely declined refreshment.

"So," he said, "we shall get right to business. A friend who works with the local constabulary tells me you reported a shooting on the beach near Piedras Rojas last night."

"Yes," Liz replied cautiously, "I did."

"According to this friend, you saw a man floating in the surf."

"That's correct."

His gaze locked with hers across the glass coffee table. "That man was my nephew."

Liz searched his eyes for some sign of pain or grief. If he was feeling either, it didn't show. Still, she offered her condolences.

"I'm sorry for your loss."

"It is my sister who weeps."

Another shiver danced along Liz's spine. If she remembered correctly, sharks were cold-blooded fish who often ate their young.

"You told the police you did not see who shot Martín?" Alvarez commented.

"That's right. I was some way down the beach. I heard the shots and ran to see what happened."

"You are very brave to run toward the sound of gunfire," he said slowly. "Or very foolish."

Liz had already decided B was the correct answer. Devlin had the right idea. She should have disappeared into the night.

"There was another man," Alvarez said, as if reading her mind. "An Americano. You did not tell the police his name."

"I didn't know it. We bumped into each other just a few seconds before we heard the shots and never got around to introductions."

It was the truth, as far as it went. She and Devlin hadn't gotten around to names *last night*. Resisting the urge to swipe her palms on her jeans-clad thighs, Liz waited for Alvarez to rephrase the question and ask if she had any idea as to the American's identity. Instead, he knocked her completely off balance with a cool remark.

"I understand you have taken a loan with Citibank for $20,000 to make a down payment on a helicopter. The fourth payment on that loan is due in three days."

Liz didn't bother to ask how the heck this guy knew her personal financial arrangements. She suspected he was supremely unconcerned about such things as confidentiality laws.

"Tell me exactly what you saw on the beach, Ms. Moore. If it helps me to locate my nephew's killer, I shall wipe out that debt for you."

"What?"

Liz sucked in a breath. An image of the Sikorsky streaked into her head. Six hundred and fifty horsepower of lift. Low noise factor, almost no vibration. Luxury leather seats for the passengers. Enough avionics to make even the most seasoned pilot drool.

The chopper would be hers. All hers. She could thumb her nose in Donny's and Bambang's faces. All she had to do was reiterate what she told the police, give this guy Devlin's name and let him squeeze what information he could out of the roustabout.

Liz had no idea what held her back. Maybe it was the thought of wading deeper into a swamp she might never slog out of. Or the utter lack of familial concern in Alvarez's black eyes.

"I told the police exactly what I saw."

"Tell me. I wish to hear it from you."

"There was a shot. No, two shots. The man, the Americano, shoved me down. Then he got up and ran in the direction of the gunfire. I followed and saw him standing over what looked like a body. Then I ran for my car to get my cell phone and call the police."

"The Americano was standing over the body?"

"That's right."

Alvarez touched fingertip to fingertip and rested his chin on the steeple. Seconds slid by, stretching Liz's nerves wire thin.

"My nephew was carrying something that belonged to me, Ms. Moore. Something that was not on his body, according to the police. I want it back."

Any inclination, however slight, to tell Alvarez about Joe Devlin evaporated at that point. The man didn't give a crap about his nephew. Just this piece of property, whatever it was.

"I didn't take anything off your nephew, if that's what you're suggesting. I waited up by my vehicle for the police to arrive. I never got close to the body."

The Shark said nothing for another second or two. Just studied her with those black predator's eyes.

"I want you to think very hard. Is there any detail you might have missed? Some bit of information that would enable me to locate this item?"

This guy was creeping her out. Somehow Liz managed a shrug. "I've told you everything I saw or heard."

He kept her pinned by that unblinking gaze for several more moments, then gave a curt nod.

"Very well. The offer stands, however. If you should think of some detail that enables me to find Martín's killer and this property I mentioned, I will pay off your loan. Juan, show Ms. Moore to her car, if you please."

Liz drove back to Piedras Rojas in a puddle of sweat, torn between relief that she'd survived her meeting with The Shark and the dead certainty that this mess wasn't over.

"Damn you, Devlin! I hope I don't live to regret covering your ass."

That worry was still hovering at the back of her mind two days later when a delivery van drove up to Aero Baja's operations center. Liz signed for the package and sought out AB's chief mechanic.

"Let's gas up the Ranger, Jorge. This is the back-ordered medicine Doc Metwani needs. It's marked priority, so I'm going to fly it out to the patch."

"Have you checked weather? There is a front forming."

"I saw it. They're forecasting thirty-knot winds with eight- to twelve-foot seas. I should be able to make it out and back before things get too bad."

Or at least make it out. If necessary, Liz could tie down and ride out the storm. It wouldn't be the first night she'd spent on the rig, or probably the last. And, she thought with a combination of anticipation and determination, an overnighter would give her a chance to have a nice long chat with a certain roughneck.

Ducking into the tiny cubicle laughingly referred to as the pilot's lounge, she spun the combination on her locker and traded her jeans and T-shirt for Aero Baja's mud-brown flight suit. The civilian clothes went into her gear bag, along with a plastic bag of toiletries.

She spent the first half of the flight thinking about the questions she wanted to ask Devlin, the second fighting the storm that blew up faster and fiercer than the forecasters had predicted. Rain lashed the windshield, the ceiling dropped to two hundred feet and the winds were a bitch by the time the LO waved Liz down and the skids touched.

The rig's tie-down crew was waiting in their bright red vests. While Liz completed the shut-down sequence, the crew secured the helo and extended the retractable hangar. Once her aircraft was protected from the elements, Liz ducked out of the rain and now howling wind.

"Looks like you'll have to ride out the storm with us tonight," the rig's quartermaster said as he signed for the medicine.

"Looks like."

"You know where the guest quarters are. Pick a bunk and make yourself comfortable."

Liz stowed her gear bag in the room set aside for transients and made a quick visit to the head before navigating the narrow corridors to the

galley. It was just after shift change, so the first
rotation was chowing down. The babble of conversations carried on in a half-dozen different languages rose above the thump, thump, thump of the
rig's heartbeat.

Liz scanned the thirty or so men and handful of
women present. She didn't spot the wide-shouldered
American she sought, so she approached the big,
brawny Irishman who'd rotated out to the patch with
him. The driller looked up with a cheerful smile on
his face as she approached.

"Back so soon, lass?"

"Had to deliver some medicines Doc Metwani
needed. I'm looking for Joe Devlin. Have you seen
him?"

"He was late coming off the deck. He's probably
still in his cabin cleaning up."

She could wait. Or she could get some answers out
of him in private. Liz chose option two.

Retracing her steps, she traversed the monstrous
recreation/entertainment center that constituted the
rig's social hub. Long hallways led off in both direc-
tions. Devlin's cabin was in the officers' wing and
had only his name on the plate beside the door. Liz
eyed the brass plate with its slip-in label thoughtfully.

Like the military and most other large organiza-
tions, offshore rigs operated under a strict hierarch-
ical structure. Petroleum engineers planned and
supervised overall operations. Drilling superinten-
dents were in charge of the deck crews, which con-

sisted of four or five drillers, derrick operators and the roughnecks who muscled the pipe into place. Less skilled roustabouts performed general maintenance tasks. Then there were the pumpers, acidizers, sample takers, welders, electricians and machinists, along with a support team that included the rig's officers, radio operators, cooks, barge operators and a medical contingent.

That Devlin rated private quarters meant he ranked fairly high in the organizational structure. Impressed despite herself, Liz rapped on the door and got a muffled shout in response.

"It's open!"

Once inside, she was greeted with the splash of running water and a gruff call from the head.

"Hang loose. I'll be right out."

She used the interval to take a quick look around. His cabin was like all the others on the rig, just a little more spacious. The built-in lockers, bunk, desk and chair were compliments of the American-Mexican Petroleum Company. So were standard-issue items that littered the cabin. A hard hat and safety goggles sat on the desk. Steel-toed boots were positioned beside the chair. A set of grease-stained overalls lay in a discarded heap, waiting to be stuffed into the laundry bag hanging from the locker handle.

Since the crews rotated every twenty-eight days and space was at a premium, they generally brought few personal items besides tools, photos and the occasional CD player, iPod, or laptop. Devlin's was a sleek, titanium-encased model that raised instant envy in Liz's breast.

Drawn by the brilliant screensaver images flashing across the liquid crystal display, she nudged a hip against the desk. But it was the Beanie bear propped next to the computer that snagged her attention. The poor guy looked as though he'd gone a few rounds with a real live grizzly and come out the loser. One ear had been torn and restitched by hand. His button eyes didn't match. The red ribbon around his neck must have once formed a neat bow, but the ends now hung limp and ragged and stained.

Interesting, Liz thought. She'd checked the next-of-kin information Devlin had provided before she'd flown him out to the patch. He'd listed a brother in Oklahoma. No wife or kids. And he certainly hadn't struck Liz as the type to tote along a childhood toy to keep him company for a month.

"So who did you belong to?" she asked, lifting the sad-eyed bear until they were nose to nose.

"The son of a friend."

The gruff reply spun Liz around. Devlin stood framed in the door to the bathroom, his chest bare. A flat, hard belly showed above the waist of his low-riding jeans. His hair was still wet and tobacco brown from his shower. His hazel eyes registered something that looked very close to suspicion.

"What are you doing here?"

It wasn't the greeting she'd expected. Particularly after the kiss this guy had laid on her back in Piedras Rojas.

"I want to talk to you."

Moving with the same, pantherlike grace that had struck her that night on the beach, he crossed the cabin, removed the bear from her hand and returned it to its comfortable slouch against the laptop. His expression wasn't particularly friendly when he faced her again.

"What about?"

Liz didn't understand *or* appreciate his attitude. Folding her arms, she gave him a saccharine smile.

"How about the fact that two thugs forced me to drive at gunpoint to the house of a seriously unnice guy? Turns out that floater you found was the nephew of El Tiburón."

His brows slashed into a quick frown. Obviously, he'd heard of The Shark.

"Are you okay?"

"I'm here, aren't I?"

Still frowning, he caught her chin and tipped her face from side to side. Checking for bruises, Liz assumed, and was immediately irritated by the heat his touch generated. So irritated she almost forgot the promise she'd made back in Piedras Rojas.

Almost.

"You don't listen very well, do you, cowboy?"

The sudden widening of his eyes told Liz he got the message a mere second or two before she brought her knee up. Devlin deflected the nut-cruncher just in time and took the jab on the tender inside of his thigh instead.

She saw his jaw lock, saw the muscle that jumped in one cheek and braced herself for some form of retaliation. It didn't come.

Liz had to admit the control he exerted over himself was impressive as hell. And just a little scary. His hazel eyes shot bullets, but he subdued the beast within and backed off with just a pained grunt.

"Damn, woman! You pack some punch with that knee."

"I warned you," Liz said coolly.

"Yeah, you did."

Eyeing her with a combination of wariness and respect, he took the conversation back to the precontact stage. "What did The Shark want with you?"

"Two things. His main concern was locating some object his nephew supposedly had with him when he died. It didn't show up among the possessions the police returned."

Devlin forgot about the spiking ache on the inside of his thigh. His botched rendezvous had suddenly taken on another twist.

OMEGA control had briefed him on the corpse's identity. Martín Alvarez had racked up a five-page rap sheet but had managed to beat every charge from drug trafficking to running prostitutes to shooting a farmer's entire litter of pigs just for the fun of hearing them squeal. Devlin was sorry he hadn't put that bullet between the goon's eyes himself.

He ran a quick mental inventory of the items he'd found during his search of the body. Martín had been carrying nothing of any significance besides that roll of pesos. Was that what The Shark wanted back? The money?

Devlin didn't think so. He'd received a thorough area brief before this op. He knew El Tiburón controlled the crime on this entire stretch of the coast. That wad of pesos wouldn't even constitute pocket change for the man.

Glancing up, Devlin caught Liz studying him with more than a trace of suspicion. "I didn't lift anything off the body," he said flatly.

"Someone did."

"Maybe it was the man who shot him. Or the police. Or someone in the coroner's office. Or you," he tacked on.

A shudder rippled through her. "Trust me on this. If I'd helped myself to a souvenir of that night, I would have returned it during my visit to Casa Alvarez."

Devlin's conscience did some serious pinging. He still regretted melting into the night and leaving this woman holding the bag. Looked like that bag was bigger and heavier and dirtier than either of them had anticipated.

"You said The Shark wanted two things. What was the second?"

"The name of the Americano who was with me that night."

Well, hell! Talk about your botched operations. This one had already gotten off to a shaky start. Devlin had a feeling it was about to completely blow apart. The Shark wouldn't swallow the story he'd fed Liz about going out to buy stolen tools.

"Did you give him my name?"

"No."

"Why not?"

"Damned if I know. But El Sharko offered me some serious bucks for information leading to the recovery of this object, whatever it is."

Her chin angled. Her brown eyes speared into him. Devlin was wondering how the hell the woman could look so belligerent and so kissable at the same time when she laid matters on the line.

"We're talking *very* big bucks here. I might just do some name dropping unless you tell me the truth about why you were on that beach."

So much for her swallowing the stolen-tool story! Devlin wouldn't make the mistake of underestimating this woman again. Going with his instincts, he told her as much of the truth as he could.

"I went to meet an informant."

Four

"Informant?"

Liz chewed on her lower lip and processed that for several seconds. A dozen possibilities kicked around inside her head. Some put Joe Devlin on the side of the good guys. Some left the issue in serious doubt.

"Was Martín Alvarez the informant you were going to meet?"

"No. As far as I know, Alvarez was an uninvited visitor to the scene. The theory is he spooked my guy, who proceeded to plug him between the eyes and disappear."

"The theory, huh?"

Liz was feeling goosier by the second. Red warning flares shot off like rockets. Her sensible, cautious inner self shouted at her to turn around and leave now, before she got in any deeper. Trouble was, she rarely listened to her sensible, cautious self. If she did, she wouldn't be saddled with an absent ex-fiancé, a bitch of a debt and the memory of El Sharko's flat, black eyes drilling into her.

"I think you'd better start at the beginning, Devlin. I want to know who you are and why you're on this rig."

"This could take a while. What time are you scheduled to make the return flight?"

"Guess you haven't stuck your head outside in the past hour or so. A good-size front has moved in. My aircraft and I are hangared in for the night."

Liz tossed the information off without thinking. Devlin's response was slower and almost as annoying as the speculation that leaped into his eyes.

"Is that so?"

Dammit! How could the man make her skin prickle with just a few drawled syllables?

"Yes, that's so." She tapped a foot. "Anytime you're ready, cowboy."

His gaze went past her. The speculation went out of his face, replaced by a hard edge. Liz looked to one side and saw he'd fixed his sights on the ragged Beanie bear.

"I told you that belongs to the son of a friend of mine," he said. "She was engaged to another friend. Harry Johnson."

"Was?"

"Harry rotated off an AmMex rig several months ago. He never made it home."

Liz scoured her mind. She ferried men back and forth every week. A few of the more gregarious—and more obnoxious—stood out in her memory. She didn't remember a Harry Johnson fitting into either category.

"Was he on this patch?"

"He was on AM-251, further south."

She knew the rig. Smaller than 237, it was serviced by one of Aero Baja's competitors.

"What happened to your friend?"

"No one knows. He disappeared."

Liz digested that information with an internal wince. "You said he was engaged. Men have been known to change their minds about little inconsequential matters like marriage. I speak from experience, you understand."

The hard edges of Devlin's face softened for a second or two. "Yeah, I got that impression the other night. Your fiancé must be a real jerk."

"Ex-fiancé, and you won't get any argument from me on that. Back to your friend. I still don't understand. If you're looking for information about him, why are you working here instead of 251?"

"Because agents from the San Diego FBI office busted a man using Harry's name and passport a few weeks ago. The bastard was running nine- and ten-year-olds across the border and selling them to brothels."

Liz zinged a glance at the Beanie bear. How awful

that a vicious child abuser would steal the identity of a man about to acquire a young son through marriage. His fiancée must have died when she heard about it.

"We now know at least two other AmMex crew members have disappeared under similar circumstances," Devlin said, his voice tight. "Both were single, with no close relatives to report them missing. Harry was pretty quiet about his personal life. Only a handful of his friends knew he was dating Evie, let alone that he'd asked her to marry him. We suspect he was targeted for that reason. We also suspect whoever fingered him operates off this rig."

"Why?"

He raked a hand through his hair and frowned at the water that dripped from his fingers. He must have forgotten he'd just stepped out of the shower. With half an acre of male chest staring her in the face, Liz was all too conscious of that minor detail.

"The informant I was meeting that night on the beach supposedly knew someone willing to supply U.S. passports for the right price. He hinted the seller was local. Our information suggests he or she also had direct access to AmMex personnel."

He didn't put any particular emphasis on the feminine pronoun, but it hit Liz like a marline spike.

"Whoa! You don't think *I* was out the on the beach to sell stolen passports, do you?"

"We considered the possibility," he admitted without a trace of apology. "The background investigation we ran on you suggested otherwise. That," he added, hooking one brow, "and the vow I over-heard you make."

"You're not ever going to let me forget that, are you?"

His grin slipped out, quick and all male. "What do you think?"

"I think I'll choose a more private setting the next time I let rip," Liz muttered before latching onto his previous statement. "You keep saying 'our' and 'we.' Are you working this problem for AmMex or someone else?"

"Let's just say a few top officials at AmMex know why I was hired on for this rotation."

Lord, he was slippery! Liz wasn't sure she believed him even now. Before she could quiz him further, however, a heavy fist pounded on his cabin door. He opened it to a roustabout in a hard hat and soaked AmMex coveralls.

The deckhand's glance widened when he spotted Liz, but the apparent urgency of his mission shifted his attention right back to Devlin. "Castlemaine needs you on the drill deck. The heavy seas are torquing line number two."

"Hell!" Whirling, Devlin snagged a clean set of overalls from a locker. "This could take a while," he said to Liz. "You want to wait here?"

"I'll grab something to eat and hang with the guys for a while. If you're too late, you can find me in the transient quarters."

She left him dragging on the overalls and returned

to the galley for a late dinner. She had to fight to keep her coffee from sloshing into her plate of curried rice and chicken before staggering down the hall toward the crew lounge. At the far end she spotted a surprised Conrad Wallace.

"What are you doing here?" the AmMex rep asked, shouldering the walls as he navigated the narrow corridor.

"I delivered the medicine Doc Metwani had on back order."

Wallace's lips pinched. Liz had no doubt he was calculating the fuel costs of an unscheduled flight. Tough. She was in no mood for one of his long-winded lectures.

"I'm flying out in the morning," she said, squeezing past his bulk. "Let me know if you have any mail or reports to ferry back."

The front seemed to settle right over the rig. Rain pounded the deck and waves crashed against the four giant columns. The rig's ever-present creaking rose in both pitch and volume until it sounded an unceasing chorus.

Inured to the groaning and creaking, off-duty crew members were engrossed in a movie in the rec center and invited Liz to join them. She enjoyed the action sequences, but the sex was a little too over the top for her tastes. She left the men to their semiporn and retreated to the transient quarters to wait for Devlin.

After a quick shower, she slipped into her favorite T-shirt, tossed her jeans over a nearby chair and stretched out on her bunk. Like most pilots, she'd trained herself to sleep in odd places at irregular hours. She intended just a quick nap, the kind of light doze that usually satisfied her body's immediate needs. She didn't count on the swaying motion of the rig, however. Within moments she was rocked into total unconsciousness.

She had no idea how long she'd been out when someone rapped on the cabin door. "Whoizzit?"

"Devlin."

Still half-asleep, she fumbled for the door lock. Her semiconscious brain registered little more than the fact that he'd shed his coveralls and now wore the shirt he'd been missing when she'd surprised him in his cabin a while ago. The well-washed denim looked as soft as cotton.

"Did you get line two untorqued?"

He didn't answer for several moments. It took Liz that long to connect his silence with the fact that she'd forgotten to pull on her jeans. Her first hint was the slow trip his gaze made from the hem of her T-shirt to her bare feet. Her second, his husky drawl.

"Two's untorqued. Can't say the same for myself at the moment."

Fully awake now, Liz tried hard for irritation. With her skin tingling everywhere his glance touched, though, all she could manage was a half-hearted indignation.

"Oh, for pity's sake! Get a grip, cowboy. I'm covered from neck to midthigh."

"Not a problem." Closing the door behind him, he flicked the lock. "We can remedy that quick enough."

The glint in his eyes clogged Liz's breath. She crossed the room with the vague intention of putting some space between them. "Careful," she warned. "Remember what happened last time you didn't ask first?"

"I remember."

He strolled across the cabin and propped both hands on the upper bunk, caging Liz between them. None of their body parts made contact. They didn't need to. His heat seemed to arc across those few inches, searing her through the thin cotton of her T-shirt.

"Permission to come aboard, Captain?"

Liz pulled in another breath, this one flavored with the tang of the saltwater glistening on Devlin's skin. She could think of a hundred reasons to refuse his request. She didn't really know this man, wasn't sure she believed everything he'd told her. And she sure as hell didn't want to get dragged any deeper into this dangerous business he hinted at.

Yet she couldn't deny he acted on her like a spark plug. Every time he got close, he transmitted an electrical energy that fired Liz's internal engine. She could feel her skin warming. Her pulse was revving faster than a main rotor at full throttle. Still, she was pretty sure she would have denied his request if the rig had remained stable.

It didn't pitch much. Only a few degrees. Just

enough to send Liz staggering forward a step, smack into Devlin's denim-covered chest.

He kept one hand anchored on the upper bunk. His other arm whipped around her waist. A slow smile spread across his face, creasing the tanned skin, crinkling the white lines at the corners of his eyes.

"I'll take that as a yes," he said, the laughter in his voice edged with a husky note that had Liz's toes curling into the deck.

She could have ended it there. Knew he'd back off if she said the word. To her profound disgust, she couldn't push out a single syllable.

She wanted this. The feel of his arms around her. The sudden heat bubbling in her blood. Had wanted it since the night on the beach, when he'd appeared out of the darkness and tempered her anger and her hurt with his cocky grin and outrageous offer.

Liz had all of two seconds to wonder if she'd lost her mind before he tightened his arm, bent his head and covered her mouth with his. She'd question her sanity later, she decided, when she got back to dry land. Right now her world had narrowed to the deck rocking beneath her feet and the solid male overwhelming her senses.

She could feel him against every inch of her body. Hear the catch to his breath as his mouth moved over hers. See the hunger that stretched his skin taut across his cheeks when he worked her T-shirt up to bare her breasts.

"I've pictured you like this a dozen times since we met," he said, his voice rough.

Since they'd met only a few nights ago, the gruff admission stroked Liz's ego even as his hand stroked her eager flesh. His callused palm was rough against her skin, his thumb gentle and incredibly skilled as it teased her nipple. The sensations streaked straight from her breast to her belly. Her vaginal muscles tightened, producing another set of sensations.

Liz's breath was coming hard and fast when she decided it was time to level the playing field. With her blood pounding and her nerve endings snapping, she attacked the buttons of his shirt.

"You know this is crazy," she muttered as she traced the contours of his shoulders and biceps with her palms. He gave a little grunt when one palm slid south, inside the waistband of his jeans.

"Yeah, I know."

His hands were all over her. Liz's locked around the length of steel poking at her belly. Sliding her fingers to the base of his shaft, she toyed with his taut sac before retracing a path along his hot, smooth length to the tip.

She was thinking that he more than lived up to the oil rig crews' reputations for supersize derricks when he shed the rest of his clothes and rid her of hers. Locked together, they tumbled to the lower bunk. Unlike the bunks aboard navy vessels, these were long and wide enough to sleep the roughnecks who regularly muscled thousand-pound lengths of pipe into place.

Thank God!

Liz was no shrimp herself. Together, she and Devlin filled the confined space between the bunks. Which made for some *extremely* stimulating friction as they traded kiss for kiss and tongue for tongue. Then his hand cupped her mound and his fingers found her slick flesh. Parting the folds, he played with her hard, tight nub.

Within moments Liz was ready to fly. She hooked a leg over his, straining against him. He got the message.

"Okay," he panted, groping for the jeans lying on the floor next to the bunk. "All right. Just hang tight a sec."

As if Liz could do anything else! His shoulder squashed hers into the mattress. His knee was wedged between her thighs. Using an elbow for leverage, he propped himself up to wrestle a condom out of its package and onto his straining flesh.

Liz observed his contortions with a wry smile. "Planned ahead, did you?"

"Yes, ma'am." His grin was fast and unrepentant as he repositioned himself between her thighs. "I told you. I've been thinking about this since the night we met."

If she hadn't believed him before, she certainly did now. With his body poised above hers, and every inch of her skin pulsating with anticipation, she could hardly do otherwise. She was ready when he eased into her, wet and welcoming when he sank home.

Devlin took it slow. *Very* slow. His blood was pounding with the force of a rotary drill boring through solid rock and his body had pretty much taken over from his brain. If he didn't keep the pace deliberate, he'd blow like an uncapped West Texas gusher.

The small corner of his rational mind that still functioned kept insisting Liz was right. This was crazy. Downright stupid, in fact. With everything else coming down, he should have put this woman out of his head days ago.

But she was lodged like a burr inside his skull. Her and that ridiculous vow. Every time Devlin had thought about it, he regretted all over again not being able to take her up on that rash vow. He also got hard as hell imagining what would have happened if he had.

Now she was here, beneath him, smooth and sleek and responsive to his every move. Devlin intended to do his damnedest to make sure *she* had no cause for regrets.

Then she clenched her muscles and he forgot about taking it slow. Forgot how insane this was. Forgot everything but the need to drive into her wet heat.

The storm peaked just after midnight. Liz did, too, when Devlin nudged her awake for a second round. She was on her side, her back to his front. He used the position to best advantage, merely wedging her leg up with one of his and coming into her from behind.

They pistoned and plunged, back to belly, thigh slapping thigh. Liz felt the top of her head almost come off with the force of her orgasm, then fell asleep again spooned against his body, his arm draped over her waist like an anchor.

She wouldn't have believed she could zone out so completely, wedged into a single bunk with a male of Devlin's size, but when she woke once more and squinted at her watch, she let out a squawk.

"Good Lord! It's almost nine."

"So?" Devlin rumbled in her ear.

"You might be on a twelve-on, twelve-off shift, but I'm not. I need to check the weather, see if I have anything or anyone to ferry back to shore, and haul ass."

She slithered out from under his weight and into the T-shirt she scooped up from the floor. Morning-afters were always awkward, this one especially so. She and Devlin weren't just casual acquaintances. They were involved to differing degrees in some pretty nasty stuff.

Tugging the hem of the shirt down to midthigh, Liz rocked on the balls of her feet. "Look, about this business with El Tiburón…"

"I'll take care of The Shark. You stay clear of him."

Her brows shot up. Devlin lay naked under the tangled sheet, his head propped on his hands, his sun-bleached brown hair standing in short spikes. He looked lazy and relaxed. His tone was anything but.

"It wasn't my idea to get up close and personal with the man in the first place," she replied with a touch of acid. "I'm curious, though. How, exactly, do you plan to take care of him? You're stuck out here on the patch for at least another three weeks."

Tossing the sheet aside, he rolled out of the bunk. When he turned to shag his jeans, Liz got a great view of shoulders roped with hard muscle; a long, tapered back and world-class buns.

The view was just as good when he faced her. The bristles on his cheeks and chin were the same golden brown as the scattering of chest hair that arrowed toward his hard, flat belly. Battling the ridiculous urge to trail a fingernail down that tantalizing line, Liz folded her arms and waited for his response.

"The how isn't important," he told her. "Just trust me on this, okay?"

"Oh, that's good coming from the man who decamped and left me to explain a dead body to the police."

"Sorry 'bout that." He scraped a palm over his bristles, his smile rueful. "It won't happen again."

"What? Me explaining a dead body or you decamping?"

Devlin kept his smile in place, but her tart comment hit home. Like most rig men, he'd made a career of going wherever the job took him. He'd lost a wife to the long separations. He had no business making promises he might not be able to keep. But he *would* ensure Liz was safe before he departed the scene again.

Crossing the few feet separating them, he curled a knuckle under her chin. "Someone will contact you within the next eight to ten hours. They'll tell you Rigger sent them."

"And Rigger is?"

"That's me, darlin'."

He dropped a kiss on her nose and scooped up the rest of his clothes. The taste of her was still on his lips when he entered his cabin, flipped up his cell phone and activated the secure satellite link to OMEGA control.

Five

"I want someone on her, and fast."

The grim urgency in Rigger's voice bled through his controller's headset. Andrew MacDonald, code named Riever, after the fierce warriors who'd roved the borderlands between Scotland and England, acknowledged the request.

"I hear you."

"This El Tiburón is one bad piece of work. We don't have proof he's involved in this stolen passport ring, but he's sure to have his hands in it somehow. He's got them in everything else down here."

Drew shot a quick glance at the electronic status board that dominated one wall of OMEGA's control center. Four operatives including Rigger were already in the field. Another was undergoing an intensive course in Arctic survival. Yet another was sporting a full leg cast, compliments of the crowbar wielded by the slasher she'd recently taken down.

Drew had already coordinated with the CIA and U.S. customs for undercover operatives to conduct additional screening of crews coming off the various AmMex rigs scattered along the Baja peninsula. He'd have to scramble to get someone down to Piedras Rojas to cover Elizabeth Moore.

"Okay, Rigger, I'll work it and get back to you."

Twenty minutes later Drew took the elevator to the first floor. He made a quick scan of the closed-circuit surveillance screen before exiting the elevator. The chief's executive assistant had already cleared him for access, but someone might have just walked in off the street. Every agent exercised great caution when leaving OMEGA's secure facilities and entering the domain of the president's special envoy.

The grandmotherly figure seated behind an ornate Louis XV reception desk greeted him with a smile. Nothing in Elizabeth Wells's neat appearance or guileless blue eyes gave any hint that she regularly qualified at the expert level with the 9 mm SIG-Sauer secreted in a special compartment in her desk.

"Go right in, Riever. Lightning is waiting for you."

"Thanks."

When she buzzed Drew into the inner sanctum, he saw that Nick Jensen wore his business uniform this morning. Drew had no doubt the tie was silk, the shoes Italian and the gray pinstriped suit made by the hand of a master tailor. He knew Lightning's cover required a patina of sophistication. He also knew the chief was as deadly with a switchblade and garrote as he was with a Beretta, which made him an all-round ace in the estimation of OMEGA's stable of operatives.

"I've been working Rigger's request for cover for Elizabeth Moore," Drew told his boss. "He wants someone on her 24/7."

"Who have you got?"

He and Nick had their heads together, going over the list of possibles, when the intercom buzzed. Moments later Maggie Sinclair Ridgeway, code name Chameleon, breezed into the inner office.

"Hi, guys."

As always, Maggie brought her own high-charged energy field with her. The sheer force of her personality and bright, engaging smile affected the two men in different ways. Nick had first encountered her on the French Riviera years ago, during a mix-up of identities with a high-priced call girl. Drew had met her only after joining OMEGA but was in awe of her legendary exploits. The fact that she'd brought Adam Ridgeway, OMEGA's sophisticated and coolly ruthless former director, to his knees only added to her mystique.

Now the mother of three children and a tenured linguistics professor at Georgetown University, she juggled kids, pets and the demands of her husband's current chairmanship of the International Monetary

Fund with equal skill. The years had put a few character lines at the corners of her brown eyes, but nothing could dim their sparkle.

"Sorry to interrupt," she said with a peck on the cheek for both of them. "I just wanted to drop off some last-minute instructions for Nick."

When Lightning gave her a blank stare, she waggled her forefinger back and forth with vigorous determination.

"Oh, no! Feigning ignorance won't work. No way I'm letting you and Mackenzie out of babysitting for us this weekend."

"Is that *this* weekend?"

"Yes, it is. Adam and I have reservations at a resort in the White Mountains," she informed Drew. "We're going to hole up for two and a half days of uninterrupted bliss. Unless Nick and Mackenzie fink out on us," she added with a speaking glance at one of the potential finks.

Nick swallowed a groan. Even with a part-time nanny and a live-in housekeeper to assist, an entire weekend at the Ridgeway residence would require fortitude, endurance and protective body armor.

The kids were okay. Pretty darn terrific, in fact. And Nick had a soft spot for the Hungarian sheepdog Maggie had inherited after doubling for the vice president. The shaggy beast's sudden growl had provided the split second of warning necessary to save both Nick and Mackenzie from a vicious spray of gunfire by hired assassins.

It was Maggie's orange-and-purple-striped pet iguana that required constant vigilance. The damned thing had a yard-long tongue and the temperament of a pit bull with a thorn stuck in its muzzle. Nick and Mackenzie had driven home from the Ridgeways' more than once decorated with iguana spit.

"You're not going to try and weasel out, are you?" Maggie demanded, something close to desperation in her eyes. "You *did* promise. And you and Mackenzie *are* Tank's godparents."

The nickname produced a reluctant smile. All OMEGA operatives used code names when in the field. After considerable discussion, they'd unanimously agreed on Tank as a handle for Maggie and Adam's two-year-old son. The kid bubbled with energy and charged joyously at every obstacle, producing enough steam to bulldoze through a brick wall.

"I don't want to weasel out," Nick lied, "but Rigger's requested additional surveillance. Drew thinks he should go himself, which means…"

"…you'll have to bring someone else in to act as Rigger's controller and personally get them up to speed on the situation," Maggie finished glumly.

She knew how heavily tasked OMEGA's agents were. She should. She'd served as both a field operative and acting head of the agency for a few years. Brow knit, she tapped a forefinger against her lower lip.

"Rigger's working that op in Baja, right? Down at the tip of the peninsula?"

"He is, but don't get any ideas. Adam will skin me alive if you decide to help us here at the control center instead of joining him for a weekend of uninterrupted bliss."

"Actually, I was thinking of combining business and bliss." Her brown eyes gleaming, Maggie dug in her purse and extracted a cell phone. "There's a world-class resort just north of Cabo San Lucas. The Two Dolphins. Adam and I have talked several times about vacationing there."

"Maggie . . ."

"We're all packed. He's on his way home from the office as we speak. We could jump on a plane in a couple of hours. Given the time difference, we should touch down in Cabo San Lucas in time for dinner."

"You might want to think about this, Maggie. You might have to stay in the field longer than a weekend."

"God, I hope so!"

Her fervent prayer raised Nick's brows until he remembered how damned good she'd been. She'd given field ops up for the director's job, then traded that for motherhood and teaching. But her exploits in the field were still the stuff of legend among OMEGA operatives.

"I can manage five or six days with no problem," she said briskly. "Adam will have to rearrange his schedule, but that's doable. We'll ask Nanny to stay at the house with Mrs. Sorenson, so you and Mackenzie will have additional backup at night."

Nick made a last, feeble attempt. "Your husband might have something to say about the change in plans."

She gave him a pitying smile and punched in a speed dial number. "I'll tell Adam to meet me here so you and Drew can brief us both on the situation."

Half an hour later, the four of them were seated around the conference table.

"This," Nick said, sliding a dossier along the length of polished mahogany, "is Elizabeth Moore. She's a pilot for Aero Baja, under contract with the American-Mexican Petroleum Company. Rigger wants you to keep her under close surveillance."

Liz aimed a stream of water at the windshield of the Ranger. With the late-afternoon sun blazing down and the temperature hovering close to 110, both she and the helicopter benefited from the spray splatting against the Plexiglas.

She'd returned from the patch less than an hour ago and filed her postflight report. With nothing else to occupy her time, she'd offered to relieve Jorge of the chore of hosing the corrosive salt spray off the chopper. It was an easy task, one that left her mind free to roam. Whatever direction her thoughts started off in, however, they always banked into a steep turn and swooped back to the same point.

Joe Devlin.

Okay, it was impossible *not* to think about the man when she could still feel the effects of the night before. There was the occasional twinge from muscles unused to the kind of workout Devlin had given them. And the tender patch on her neck where his bristles had scraped. And the sudden tingle in her nipples whenever she remembered how he'd tongued them to hard, aching points.

Still, Liz couldn't quite believe she'd actually done what she'd vowed to during her ritual shredding of Donny's e-mail. She'd gotten naked with the very next man she'd met. It had taken several days and a visit to El Tiburón to make it happen, but happen it had.

Shaking her head, Liz aimed a jet stream at the forward-engine coupling. Who the heck was she kidding? She'd done a whole lot more than just get naked. She'd erupted like a modern-day Vesuvius. Both times. Devlin probably thought he'd struck oil. A hot, gushing stream of…

"Ms. Moore?"

The deep baritone sounded above the water's splash. Keeping the hose aimed at the rotor, Liz speared a glance over her shoulder.

"Yes?"

A figure stepped out of the hangar's shadow into the late-afternoon sunlight. Liz's heart did a nervous little jig until she noted he didn't walk with a limp. Nor was he wearing a purple silk shirt.

When she noted what he *was* wearing, her breath slid back down her throat. She hadn't been this close to such sophisticated masculinity since… Well. Never.

Devlin and the other oilmen she ferried out and back from the rig were brawny and tough and all male. This guy was Pierce Brosnan classed up several notches, if that was possible. Elegantly casual in a parrot-print polo shirt, pleated khaki slacks and tasseled loafers, he sported jet-black hair touched with silver at the temples and eyes a clearer and more compelling blue than the Pacific.

"The man I spoke to at the operations center—I think his name was Jorge Garcia—said I'd find you here. I'm Adam Ridgeway."

Shutting off the spray, Liz swiped her wet palm on her flight suit and returned his no-nonsense grip. "What can I do for you, Mr. Ridgeway?"

"My wife and I are staying at the Two Dolphins. The concierge told us Aero Baja does charter flights. We're thinking of buying some vacation property here and would like to hire you to show us the coast."

"Aero Baja does charters, but we have to schedule them around our flights for the American-Mexican Petroleum Company. AmMex is our bread and butter."

"No problem. All Maggie and I have to schedule around are our tee times." His penetrating blue eyes went past her to the helo. "I see you're flying the older model 214."

"She may be old, but she's got all new avionics."

"That's good to hear." A small smile played at one corner of his mouth. "Does she still drag her tail when you walk her off the pad with a full load?"

Well, well. He wasn't just a pretty face.

"Like a duck trying to take a squat," Liz admitted, making a swift mental reassessment. "Logged a few hours in a cockpit, have you?"

"A few. My wife's waiting at the office. Shall we go inside?"

Liz would have guessed the urbane Ridgeway would choose a sumptuous redhead or Chanel-draped blonde for a mate. The brunette perched on the corner of the desk looked far more intriguing. Comfortably chic in a gauzy white peasant skirt and white ribbed tank top, she'd pushed her sunglasses to the top of her head to sweep back her shoulder-length, honey-brown hair. It appeared she and Jorge had just shared some joke. Her cinnamon eyes danced with laughter and her rich chuckles suggested a woman who lived life to the fullest.

Liz liked her on the spot. She liked her even more when Ridgeway's voice deepened to a near caress.

"I see you've made yourself at home, my darling. As always."

Any woman who could evoke that husky note from a man like Adam Ridgeway had to be *very* special. Smiling, Liz held out her hand.

"Hello, Mrs. Ridgeway. I'm Liz Moore."

"Please, call me Maggie." The laughter still danced in her eyes. "Jorge's been telling me about the American who chartered you to take his family whale watching a few months back."

Liz groaned. She'd spent hours cleaning up vomit after that memorable flight. "You'd think a man with four kids prone to motion sickness would find another way to educate them about whales."

"Now, Lizetta," Jorge said with a grin, "the gringo swore he did not know their stomachs were so delicate."

"Our kids aren't with us on this trip," Maggie assured Liz. "And if they were, you wouldn't have to worry about their stomachs."

"True," her husband said with a wry smile. "Gillian would probably be hanging out the side hatch, Samantha would beg you to do loop-de-loops and Tank would want at the controls."

"Tank?"

"Our son."

"He's two," Maggie said blithely, as if that explained everything. "This is the first time we've left them for more than a day or two. Our friends are babysitting." She shared a quick glance with her husband. "I hope Nick and Mackenzie survive."

"They've got plenty of backup," Ridgeway replied calmly. "How does tomorrow afternoon look for you?" he asked Liz. "I checked the map and thought we'd head north first."

She flicked a glance at the grease board on the far wall. She wasn't scheduled to make her next run out to the rig until Tuesday. Unless she came up with an excuse to make one before then.

The thought wiggled into her head like a slippery little eel and wouldn't wiggle out. It snuggled right up to the image of Devlin sprawled in her bunk this morning. Unshaven. Smug. So damned sexy Liz wanted to climb back in and crawl all over him.

She was certifiable, she thought in disgust. Completely certifiable! One night with the man and she was already plotting another.

"Tomorrow afternoon is fine," she said crisply, "unless there's an emergency out on the rig and we have to make an unscheduled run."

"I understand we take second priority," Ridgeway replied. "Maggie and I will be out and around tomorrow morning. Here's my card with my cell phone number. Please keep it handy and call if you need to cancel."

Liz fingered the thick velum with its heavily embossed letters. They spelled out an impressive title—Adam Ridgeway, Governor pro tem, International Monetary Fund. Below that was a Washington, D.C., address.

Tugging down the zipper to her leg pocket, she extracted a plastic card case. Ridgeway's card slid in between her Baja Aero ID, her credit cards and several folded hundred-peso notes.

"We'll see you tomorrow," his wife said, slinging a straw tote over her shoulder. She abandoned her perch on the desk and started for the door. Halfway there she turned back.

"Oh, by the way… Rigger sent us."

Maggie hid a smile as Liz's brows shot up. Waggling her fingers in farewell, Maggie accompanied Adam out into the searing heat and tipped her sunglasses from the top of her head onto her nose.

"Nice going," she murmured as her husband escorted her to their rental car. "The chip embedded in your business card will allow us to track her every move."

"Amazing what they've come up with since our days," he replied, only half in jest.

"I like how you got her to tuck the card in with her ID. You haven't lost your touch."

Adam grinned down at her. "Feels good to be back in the field after all these years, doesn't it?"

"Damn good!"

Devlin got word that Chameleon and Thunder had tagged Liz shortly after he came off his twelve-hour shift. Stripping down, he hit the shower.

Chameleon and Thunder were both legends around OMEGA. Devlin knew Maggie better than Adam, having worked for her for a few months before she left to have her second child. But Ridgeway's reputation spoke for itself. Devlin couldn't have asked for better cover for Liz. Unless, of course, he provided it himself.

Grunting, he soaped down. The mere thought of all the ways he *wanted* to cover Elizabeth Moore flashed through his mind. He'd accomplished several different coverings last night. Next time he'd try a few more.

He had no doubt there would be a next time. Since meeting Liz on the beach what now seemed like a lifetime ago, he hadn't been able to get her out of his head. He'd figured their hours together in that cramped bunk would satisfy the lust she generated in him. He'd figured wrong. If anything, the feel of her sleek, supple body under his had fed a craving for more.

Her involuntary visit with Alvarez had thrown him a real curve, however. In addition to lusting after the woman, he was now worried as hell about her safety. Devlin had yet to link Eduardo Alvarez to the stolen passports. Or to his friend Harry, missing for several months. But Alvarez controlled the drug trade in this area with an iron fist. Odds were he controlled all other illegal activities. If El Tiburón had sold Harry's passport to the bastard who'd used it to run child prostitutes across the border, Devlin intended to have a piece of him.

First he had to establish the link, if there was one. They'd tracked the crew members that had rotated off the patch when Devlin had rotated on. All had arrived home safely and were still accounted for. Another batch was scheduled to rotate in three days, when Liz made her next scheduled run.

Devlin had already gotten acquainted with four of the men. He'd also planted tracking devices in their personal gear. If any of the four disappeared en route to their homes, the device might help locate them.

He had the next two days to tag the remaining two, both of whom possessed entry visas for the States. One was Portuguese and planning to visit a cousin in Massachusetts. The other hailed from Kuwait and had applied for a follow-on job at a rig off the coast of Louisiana.

Unfortunately, both men spoke limited English and Devlin's Portuguese was as fractured as his Arabic. He had the solution for the communications problem, however.

Toweling off, he dressed and dug a set of miniature earphones out of his desk drawer. The earphones were plastic, the kind that plugged into any iPod or MP3 player. Devlin unscrewed one of the tiny buds that served as an earpiece and inserted it into his ear canal before contacting Riever via his cell phone.

"Okay, Riev, I need you to sing to me in Portuguese."

"No problem, pal."

Knowing Devlin would be working with an international crew, OMEGA's electronics wizard, Mackenzie Blair, had adapted the miniaturized translator recently developed by the military for special operations forces dropped behind enemy lines. The tiny computer embedded in the earpiece used satellite signals to pick up spoken words, interpret them and feed an instant response. It wasn't as reliable as a real-live interpreter who could assess facial expressions and idiomatic nuances, of course. But absent a reliable man on the scene, the little bug worked wonders.

"Pode você ouvir-me?"

The device translated Riever's question and supplied Devlin an answer.

"Yeah, I can hear you," he replied in fluent Portuguese.

"Sounds like you're good to go."

"Roger that."

With the device buried deep in his left ear, Devlin went in search of Paulo Casimiro. He found the dark-eyed, curly-haired crane operator in the recreation center, wearing a look of desperation. Conrad Wallace had cornered the man and was expounding on a recent trip to Lisbon and the loss of a fistful of cash in the famed Estoril Casino.

"Two hundred euros," Wallace groused. "*Compreende* two hundred? That's, uh, *dos ciento*."

A quiet murmur sounded in Devlin's ear. "I think you mean *dois cem,*" he then said to the AmMex rep.

"*Dos, dois,* whatever. The point is, those dealers at the Estoril were raking in the euros faster than I could shell them out. Damned dealers had to have stacked the deck. I tell you, they—"

Ruthlessly Devlin cut him off midstream. Courtesy was wasted on Wallace.

"I need to borrow Paulo for a few moments. I understand he's rotating in two days. Before he leaves, I'd like him to show me this new computer-aided off-load system. I've heard about it, but haven't seen how it works."

It was a legitimate request. Crane operators on offshore rigs had a helluva job. The cab they worked in sat almost ninety feet above the surface of the sea, limiting their visibility. Fog, strong winds and rough seas could make the task of loading and unloading supply ships a tricky proposition at best.

At worst, the crash of a metal crane against a steel deck could spark a fire, as had happened just last year off the coast of Brazil. Almost a hundred men died in the series of explosions that followed. Three days later, exhausted rescue workers had watched with tears streaming down their faces as what remained of one of the world's largest rigs had tipped onto its side and sunk into the turquoise waters.

After that incident AmMex had followed the lead of other major oil companies and purchased a computer-based, sonar-sounding system that helped operators judge the crane's position relative to the boat deck. Besides having a professional interest in the system, Rigger figured asking about it was a good way to detach Paulo from Wallace and get him alone for a spell.

He figured right. Using pantomime and a few key phrases fed to him through his earpiece, he got his message across. The burly Paulo jumped to his feet and led the way out of the lounge. Devlin followed, making a mental note to have Riever dig into Conrad Wallace's financial situation. Losing a couple hundred euros at a casino was no big deal—as long as Wallace didn't make a habit of it.

In the meantime, Devlin had two days to get close to Paulo Casimiro.

Six

Maggie and Adam Ridgeway showed up at Aero Baja at one-fifteen the following afternoon. Liz spent the rest of the day with them, starting with a three-hour aerial tour of the coast north of Piedras Rojas and finishing with drinks at their private casita and dinner at the restaurant of their exclusive resort.

The following afternoon they flew south. A slight dogleg at Todos Santos took them to Eduardo Alvarez's walled compound. Liz made only one low-level pass. The heavily armed gate guards didn't appear to appreciate the outside interest. The two goons had their semiautomatics at shoulder level when Liz zoomed away.

"Interesting," Maggie commented through the

headset, twisting around in her seat harness to get another look at the compound.

"Very," Adam agreed.

They made a brief stop at the resort town of Cabo San Lucas, crowded with tourists off the gleaming white cruise ships lined up at the docks. Maggie tried to convince Adam she only wanted to pick up some souvenirs for the kids, but he insisted on buying her a magnificent silver cuff incised with a lizard set in turquoise, lapis and malachite.

Once back in Piedras Rojas, Liz invited Maggie and Adam to join her for dinner at El Poco Lobo. She'd gained enough insight into the aristocratic-looking Adam by now to know he wouldn't hesitate to chow down at a chipped Formica table on Anita's chicken, frijoles and rice. Still, she was surprised at how easily he blended in. While Maggie and Liz devoured hot, cinnamon-and-sugar-dusted sopaipillas dripping with honey, Adam joined the locals at the bar. Within minutes he was immersed in a deep philosophical discussion of the relative merits of football versus soccer.

Contentedly licking the honey from their fingers, Maggie and Liz lolled at their outdoor table in a breeze stirred by the swirling overhead fan. Cool and comfortable in a white cotton peasant blouse trimmed with colorful ribbons, another gauzy skirt and huarache sandals, Maggie tossed back the strong local brew with the same gusto she seemed to bring to every aspect of her life.

After two days in their company, Liz knew little

about their personal life aside from the fact that they had three children and lived in Washington, D.C. Curious, she drew a lazy circle on the Formica with her dew-streaked beer bottle. "How long have you and Adam been married?"

"Ten years next month. We worked together for some time before that. Those were, uh, interesting years." Her gaze drifted to the tall, broad-shouldered Americano at the bar. "These are better, though. *Much* better."

Ridgeway glanced over his shoulder and caught his wife's gaze. Smiling, he tipped his beer bottle in her direction. The look they shared sent a little ping of envy through Liz.

She'd been so sure she'd found her mate in Donny. Had sweated down here in Mexico all these months to build up their joint account and dreamed of buying the first of their planned fleet. All the while he was having fun with Bambang.

Bambang. God!

Her disgusted grunt brought the other woman's head around.

"Sorry. Did you say something?"

"No."

"What about you?" Maggie asked after a moment, picking up the conversational thread. "Do you have any particular males on your radar scope?"

"I had one. He dropped off a week or so ago."

Liz took a long swallow of beer and made an interesting discovery. The anger was still there, but fading fast. So was the self-disgust. But the hurt had completely evaporated. A certain roustabout had shoved Donny Carter right out of her heart.

"Another just popped up on the screen," she admitted with a half-embarrassed shrug.

Maggie arched a brow. "Would his name happen to be Joe Devlin?"

"It would." Shaking her head, Liz thumped the bottle back onto the table. "You'd think I would have learned my lesson. I fell for one slick operator and got burned. How dumb is it to jump into a bunk with another man less than a week later?"

Surprise rounded Maggie's eyes. "You and Devlin have made it to the bunk-jumping stage?"

"I didn't plan it."

"I'll bet he did!" Maggie retorted on a choke of suppressed laughter. "I know Rigger. He never goes into any situation unprepared."

Remembering the stash of condoms he'd had conveniently to hand, Liz pursed her lips. "See, that's the problem. You're obviously well acquainted with him. All I know is that he's big and tough and complicated."

"That pretty much pegs him. And most of the other men he associates with, my husband included."

Liz leaned back, letting the breeze stir the ends of the blunt-cut hair just touching her shoulder. "I don't suppose you're going to tell me exactly who you and Adam and Devlin work for."

"Adam is with the International Monetary Fund," Maggie replied gently. "As his business card indicates. I teach linguistics at Georgetown University. And Devlin is currently employed by…"

"…the American-Mexican Petroleum Company. Okay, I get the picture. I'm not cleared for that level of detail."

Drumming on the table with her nails, Liz shifted her gaze. The cantina was set on a slight hill, with red tile–roofed houses spilling down the hill on either side. Through the narrow slice between buildings she could just make out the cliffs that gave Piedras Rojas its name. The rocks glowed bright copper in the evening sun.

The scene was so peaceful, so idyllic. A small village perched on the cliffs overlooking the Pacific. A handful of cars parked in the narrow, cobbled streets. Dust swirling lazily in the slanting rays of the sun. Hardly the setting for danger and intrigue and murder.

"Devlin told me a little of what this is all about," she said, swinging her gaze back to Maggie. "It's pretty nasty stuff."

"Yes, it is."

"I might be able to help if you fill me in on…"

"*Hola,* Lizetta."

Grinning under his thick mustaches, Jorge waved and worked his way through the crowd. With him was a man Liz recognized as one of his many relatives. The fishing boat captain, she guessed from his denim shirt and the red bandanna knotted around his neck. The fishy tang of the docks that came with him provided another clue.

"Hello, Jorge. You remember Mrs. Ridgeway."

"But of course." The mechanic bowed over Maggie's hand with the grace of a matador. "Señora Ridgeway, this is my wife's cousin. I tell Emilio that Lizetta takes you and your husband up for charter flights. He wishes to know if you would like to charter his boat as well. The *Santa Guadalupe* is a very fine boat," he assured her.

"Very fine," the wiry Emilio echoed. "Clean and fast."

"We haven't talked about a fishing charter," Maggie said with a smile, "but I know Adam would enjoy it if we have time. Why don't you join us for a drink? I'll get him over to speak with you about it."

"She is a nice woman," Jorge commented as she went to relay their request for a cold beer to her husband.

"And very rich," Emilio murmured.

Liz said nothing. Tourism was the second largest legitimate industry in the area after tuna fishing. The locals could size up potential customers with a single glance at their shoes or watch. Then there was the rock atop the heavy gold band circling Maggie's ring finger….

When she returned with her husband and fresh drinks in tow, the talk turned to fish. Pacific striped marlin. Roosterfish. Sailfish. Tuna, dorado and wahoo. Liz sipped her beer, listening with half an ear, and let her thoughts slide back to her epiphany of a few moments ago. She was over Donny. She'd probably been over him for months and hadn't realized it. She ought to be grateful to Bambang.

And to Devlin.

Her thoughts turning inward, Liz hid a small smile. She'd have to show him just *how* grateful on her next run out to the patch. If she timed it right, she could catch him coming off his shift and…

"Ayyyy!"

Dismayed, Jorge made a grab for the beer bottle he'd sideswiped while demonstrating the size of one of his cousins-in-law's catches. The bottle flew off the table, spraying Maggie's blouse in the process, and hit the floor. The thick glass didn't shatter, but clinked around under the table a few times, spraying feet and shoes as well.

"*Excúse, señora! Excúse!*"

"It's okay." Smiling, Maggie raised the wet cotton a few inches off her chest. "No harm done."

"I am so clumsy," Jorge moaned as Emilio and Liz both bent to retrieve the bottle.

They came within a hair of knocking heads. She drew back just in time and left it to the fisherman to scoop up the bottle. When he did, a thin gold chain slithered out of his shirt collar. Dangling from the end of the chain was a three-inch-long shark's tooth capped with a gold filigree crown.

Liz froze, bent low in her chair. She'd seen a necklace just like that recently. Around the neck of Eduardo Alvarez, in the photo taken with his family aboard a sleek white yacht.

"That's quite a trophy," she commented. "Did it come from one of your catches?"

Emilio glanced down and muttered a curse under his breath. With a swift move, he stuffed the tooth back inside his shirt.

"*Sí,* I catch it."

Straightening, he plunked the bottle on the table and shoved back his chair.

"I must go," he told the Ridgeways. "You will contact Jorge if you wish to fish, yes?"

"Yes, we will."

While Maggie and Adam said goodbye to the still-mortified Jorge, Liz sat like a cardboard cutout in her chair. She had the sinking suspicion she'd just spotted the item of property El Tiburón was determined to reclaim.

Problem was, she couldn't decide what the heck to do about it.

She almost mentioned the tooth to Maggie and Adam before they parted at the cantina. Loyalty to Jorge kept her silent. He wasn't just her partner at work. He was her closest friend here in Mexico. She'd eaten dinner with him and Maria and their assorted relatives dozens of times and returned their hospitality at regular intervals.

She refused to believe the Aero Baja mechanic was involved in any way with the shooting on the beach. But he *had* brought Emilio to the cantina, and Emilio *had* acted really weird over the tooth.

Chewing on her lower lip, Liz drove through the

gathering dusk and parked under the leafy jacaranda tree. She kept her collapsible baton handy until she ascertained the massive trunk shielded no unwanted visitors, then climbed the stairs to her apartment.

The three rooms welcomed her with warm yellow walls and smooth tile floors. Since Liz had put every spare peso into the bank, she'd limited her decorating to inexpensive paintings by local artists and colorful handwoven rugs. Her only real indulgence was satellite Internet service.

She'd tried to convince Conrad Wallace that AmMex should cover the cost, since she used her computer to check weather the night before scheduled flights. Fiscally conservative as always, Wallace had countered that she should use the weather service at the terminal.

Tossing her purse onto the sofa, Liz hunkered down at the computer and booted up. When the screen lit up, she logged onto the net and typed "Eduardo Alvarez, El Tiburón" into Google's search box. A click of the mouse returned a surprising number of entries, but instead of scrolling through them, Liz aimed the pointer at the images icon at the top of the search screen.

She found what she was looking for almost immediately. The second image she looked at showed a black-and-white newspaper image of Alvarez. The photographer had caught him at an angle. His face was turned away, his upper torso twisted. The neck of his shirt had parted just enough to show a white triangle outlined against a mat of black chest hair.

Her stomach knotting, Liz zoomed in on the triangle. Yep, there it was, unique filigree crown and all.

She'd lived in Mexico for seven months, had hit the jewelry markets in Cabo and in La Paz. The tourists seemed to love shark's teeth necklaces, but the teeth were usually small and strung on leather rather than gold chain. Best she could recall, she'd never seen one as big or with such elaborate workmanship as this one. A master goldsmith had crafted the crown. The tooth itself…Liz didn't want to think about the size of the shark that must have come from.

Suspicion now hardened into certainty, she printed out the picture and exited the search mode. That was when she noted the envelope icon at the upper corner of her screen. Another click took her to her e-mail. One was from her mom, currently vacationing in Michigan with a gaggle of girlfriends. Another was a notice from Citibank confirming receipt of the latest payment on the loan she'd taken out for the Ranger. The third was from Donny.

Liz stared at the return address for a full minute, her finger hovering over the delete key. Finally she mouthed a gruff what-the-hell and opened the e-mail. She skimmed the lines, her jaw dropping in the process.

He'd made a mistake.

He loved her.

He wanted her to jettison the job in Mexico and fly to Malaysia on the next flight out. They'd get married as soon as she arrived.

"Right!" she hooted. "Like that's going to happen."

Fingers flying, she zinged off a pithy, two-word reply. She was still feeling the satisfaction of that terse response when she shut down the computer. The photo in the printer's tray sobered her instantly. Gnawing on her lower lip, Liz stared down into The Shark's flat, black eyes.

"Now what the heck am I going to do about you?"

After a fierce internal debate, she dug out Adam Ridgeway's card. He answered on the third ring, sounding curt, almost impatient.

"Ridgeway."

"It's Liz." She hesitated a moment, thrown off by his tone. "Did I catch you at a bad time?"

"What can I do for you?"

He'd dodged the question, but the creak of bedsprings and faint rustle of sheets provided their own answer.

Liz fought a grin. It wasn't yet nine o'clock, and Maggie and Adam had already hit the sheets. She had a pretty good hunch they hadn't been snoozing.

"I may have something, some information."

Adam's tone altered significantly. "What kind of information?"

She thought about the sophisticated electronics in Alvarez's study. And remembered that he'd known to the penny how much she owed Citibank. She wouldn't put it past him to have bugged her phone. Or have one of his goons parked down the street, manning a high-powered listening device.

"Why don't I drive over to the resort? I can be there in a half hour."

"That works."

Liz just bet it did. Guessing that the bedsprings would get a hard, fast workout, she hung up.

A quick shower removed the grime from the afternoon flight and heat of the day. Her hair still damp, Liz tucked the folded picture of El Tiburón into the back pocket of her jeans and slid her feet into flip-flops.

Night wrapped the coast road in breezy darkness. The surf foamed against the rocks, spinning lacy collars in the moonlight. What looked like a billion stars studded the sky. No clouds or storms on the horizon tonight.

Too bad, Liz thought with a wry smile. She was scheduled to ferry a replacement crew out to AM-237 first thing in the morning. She wouldn't have the excuse of a storm to delay her return flight.

The Two Dolphins Resort was perched on a curve of high cliffs some eight miles from Piedras Rojas. A spotlighted fountain with two giant bronze bottle-noses splashing joyfully marked the entrance to the resort. Flickering torches outlined the drive. With fragrant hibiscus crowding the roadside and eucalyptus trees touching branches overhead, Liz felt as though she was driving through a perfumed tunnel.

The main lodge of the resort sat in floodlit splendor at the end of the drive. From her visit the previous evening, Liz knew to circle the lodge and branch off on the graveled drive that led to Maggie and Adam's casita. Like the other bungalows at this high-priced getaway, the bougainvillea-draped cottage boasted a private pool complete with blue-and-white-striped cabana and deck overlooking the moon-washed Pacific.

One of these days, Liz thought as she parked beside the Ridgeways' rental vehicle, she might just treat herself to a vacation at a place like this. After she paid off the loan for that damned nonrefundable deposit. And reconstructed her bank account. And figured out just what the heck she was going to do when her AmMex contract came up for renewal again.

Time enough to worry about all that later. Right now the folded photo of The Shark was so hot she half expected it to burn a brand on her butt.

Soft golden light spilled from the windows of the casita. Liz crunched up the gravel path to the front door and let the dolphin-shaped brass knocker clank against the door. Maggie opened it, her hair a tousled brown cloud. She'd belted on a peach silk robe trimmed in ecru lace. The edges swished against the matching gown as she stepped aside.

"Hi, Liz. Come in."

The interior of the bungalow was as luxurious as the exterior. Her flip-flops slapping the tiles, Liz followed Maggie down a foyer lined with feathery potted ferns.

"Sorry 'bout the interruption."

"No problem. Actually, you aren't our only visitor."

Maggie swept a hand toward the male standing

beside Adam in the sitting room. Liz gaped at the unexpected sight.

"Devlin!"

"In the flesh, darlin'."

Flesh was right. Most of his was showing. Black Lyrca covered the little that wasn't. The short-sleeved muscle shirt clung to his chest and biceps like a thin coat of paint. The black shorts did the same on his muscular thighs. Both garments had obviously been designed to wear with the wet suit and scuba gear draped over a nearby chair.

"Don't tell me you swam all the way from the patch!"

"Only part of the way," he said, grinning. "I had a boat waiting."

"But…but…" Thrown for a loop by his unexpected appearance, Liz croaked like a tongue-tied macaw. "When did you get here?"

Adam answered that one. "About five minutes after you called," he said with just a hint of dryness in his aristocratic voice. "A little earlier than we expected."

He didn't look at his wife, but Maggie flushed and Devlin swallowed a snort of laughter. Still bewildered, Liz wanted more of an explanation.

"I don't understand. What are you doing here?"

"I wanted to be on hand to observe the crew rotating off the rig tomorrow morning. See where they go, who they talk to."

"So why didn't you just fly back with me when I picked them up?"

"Because we don't want them to know they're being observed," he explained. "Between us, Maggie, Adam and I are going to make sure the individuals who step off your helo are the same ones who continue into the States."

Liz was a little ticked they hadn't included her as part of the observation committee. She'd voice her opinion about that in a minute. Right now she was more curious about how the heck Devlin had orchestrated another disappearing act.

"Won't they miss you out on the patch?"

"Not unless there's an emergency. I worked a double shift yesterday. Twenty-four hours straight, with the next twenty-four off. I posted a sign in four languages on my cabin door. Anyone who knocks risks severe maiming or death. Maggie told me about your call," he said, shifting gears. "What's up?"

"This."

Reaching into her hip pocket, she extracted the printed photo and passed it to Devlin. When he unfolded the paper and recognized Alvarez's image, his brows snapped together.

"Has The Shark come after you again?"

"No. Although a couple of his resident thugs did aim Uzis my way yesterday."

Before Liz could explain about the low-level pass over Alvarez's compound, Devlin threw Ridgeway a swift glance.

"I thought you had her on a leash."

"We do."

"What leash?" Liz asked, frowning.

"Are the signals faulty? Did you lose her?"

"Hey! What leash?"

"The signals work perfectly," Adam said calmly. "Maggie and I were with her when it happened."

"What's this business about Uzis? How did…?"

Liz put her first and fourth fingers to her mouth. Her ear-shattering whistle spun Devlin around and had the other two wincing.

"*What* leash, dammit?"

Seven

Devlin had once strayed into a patch of quicksand. He'd been working a rig in a backwater Louisiana bayou at the time. The swamp was wet and boggy, crowded with marsh grasses, palmettos and moss-laden cypress trees. After stepping off a skiff onto what he thought was solid ground, he'd sunk to his kneecaps. As the echoes of Liz's shrill whistle hammered against his eardrums, he experienced the same sinking sensation.

"I was worried about you. I asked Maggie and Adam to tag you."

"Tag me how?"

Her voice was low and lethal. Bravely, Adam attempted to draw her fire.

"There's a microchip embedded in the business card I gave you. It tracks your every movement. If you'd strayed into unfamiliar or dangerous territory, one of us would have been there within minutes."

She didn't waste her fury on Adam. Turning her attention back to Devlin, she shot off so many sparks he could feel their white hot bite.

"Bastard. I actually—almost—trusted you."

Bristling, she dug a hand into the left front pocket of her jeans. Devlin kept his mouth shut when she produced a flat plastic case. Said nothing when she pulled out an embossed business card. But he almost blew it when she ripped it into halves, then quarters, and let the pieces flutter to the carpet.

Just in time he bit back the comment that she'd conducted a similar ritual the night they'd met. He didn't think Liz was in any mood to appreciate the irony.

"I want the truth this time," she demanded. "Were you three keeping tabs on me because you think I'm part of this stolen passport scheme?"

That one Devlin could answer unequivocally and without hesitation.

"No. I told you we considered the possibility. We also dedicated considerable resources to vetting you. Everything came back clean."

Her eyes narrowed to slits. "Was that what our little session in your cabin out on the rig was all about? You were 'vetting' me?"

The quicksand was up around Devlin's waist now. He could feel it sucking him deeper into the bog, but didn't look to either Maggie or Adam for help. They couldn't throw him a rope on this one.

"There's only so much I'll do for my country." That wasn't completely true, but the next statement was. "That particular session was for me and me alone."

He could see she wasn't buying it. He figured he had one last shot before he went under.

"You're smart, sexy and one hell of a pilot, Liz, but you're not in The Shark's league. I told you I was sending in some backup. You didn't object."

"Backup is one thing! Putting me under electronic surveillance without my knowledge or consent is another."

"I was worried about you," he repeated. It was his only real defense.

"Want to know what you can do with your worry?"

She hadn't given up the battle, but her voice had lost some of its steam. Relief rippled through Devlin. He might yet make it out of the swamp.

"How about we discuss that privately? After you tell us about this photograph of Alvarez."

The diversion worked, thank God. With a look that promised him some uncomfortable moments later, she stabbed a finger at the photo.

"See the necklace he's wearing?"

Maggie and Adam crowded around the picture. They made quite a trio, Liz thought as she struggled to get a grip on her temper. Adam as sleek as a panther with his black hair and half-buttoned white shirt. Maggie trim and elegant in peach silk. Devlin—the rat!—looking unrepentant and testosterone charged in that damned Lycra.

"That's a shark's tooth dangling from the chain," Liz pointed out.

"Apropos," Maggie commented as they passed the photo from hand to hand.

"You can't see the details, but a magnifying glass would show the tooth has gold filigree crown with a hook to loop a chain through. The filigree pattern is very intricate and very distinctive."

"We'll take your word for it," Devlin said. "So?"

"So I saw that same necklace tonight. On Jorge's cousin Emilio."

She speared a quick look at Maggie and Adam. Surprise and quick interest flared in their eyes. Devlin couldn't make the connection.

"Who are Emilio and Jorge?"

"Let's sit down," Adam suggested, gesturing to the love seat and easy chairs grouped around a hammered brass coffee table. "Liz can fill you in on the details."

Maggie dropped into one of the overstuffed chairs. Adam took a seat on the broad arm. Liz chose the love seat, then had to scoot over a few inches when Devlin crowded in beside her. The man tended to occupy more than his fair share of space, she thought wryly. In bed and out.

Sternly banishing the thought, she launched into an explanation. "Jorge Garcia is Aero Baja's chief mechanic. You saw him at the terminal the morning I flew you out to the patch."

He wrinkled his brow. "Short? Handlebar mustache? Grease under his fingernails?"

Amazed he could recall such detail about a man he'd glimpsed only briefly, she nodded.

"Emilio is Jorge's wife's cousin. He owns and operates a fishing boat. The *Santa Guadalupe*. Jorge brought him to the cantina to meet Maggie and Adam earlier this evening. He and his cousin-in-law thought the Rigeways might be interested in chartering the boat for some sport fishing."

"And this Emilio was wearing a shark's tooth necklace?"

"He was."

"You've got keen eyes," Maggie commented. "I didn't notice it."

"I spotted the glint of a gold chain," Adam said slowly, "but not what was attached to it."

"Remember when Jorge knocked over the beer bottle? Emilio and I both ducked down to retrieve it. The tooth slipped out of his shirt then. When I remarked on it, he got all flustered, stuffed the thing back inside his collar and—"

"—left faster than a gamecock with his tail feathers on fire," Maggie exclaimed. "Do you think this shark's tooth connects Emilio to Alvarez? Is it a gang symbol? A mark of the brothers?"

"I don't think it's a gang thing. The two goons who drove me out to Alvarez's compound weren't sporting any teeth but their own. No, this one is very distinctive." She paused for dramatic effect. "My guess is it's the personal possession El Tiburón's so anxious to recover."

She'd had plenty of time to puzzle this out during the drive to the resort.

"Alvarez told me his nephew was carrying something the night he was shot. Something that belonged to him. Something he wanted back. I'm thinking he gave the tooth to Martín. Or Martín borrowed it without his uncle's permission. Maybe he just wanted to flash it around. Maybe he was using it as a signal that he had his uncle's backing for whatever he was up to. In either case, my guess is Emilio lifted it off Martín's body. Or knows who did."

The other three exchanged glances. Their minds seemed to click on a level that didn't include Liz.

"It fits," Adam said. "Jorge works for Aero Baja. He has access to the AmMex flight manifests."

"He knows who's coming off the rig and when," Maggie murmured. "Jorge passes the information to his wife's cousin, who just happens to own a deep-sea fishing boat."

His face grim, Devlin picked it up from there. "Emilio approaches the target, takes him out on the boat, steals his passport and dumps him overboard. He then sells the passport to Alvarez, uncle or nephew. He even tries to make some extra on the side by arranging a meeting with an Americano reportedly willing to pay big bucks for information about the men coming off the rig."

His hazel eyes hardened to agate.

"I'm betting he didn't intend to tell me a damned thing. He probably arranged that midnight rendez-vous with the idea of bumping me off and lifting my papers, as well. Except something went wrong. Martín Alvarez got wind of the meeting. Followed Emilio to the beach to see what he was up to, maybe intending to take him out. But Emilio got to him first."

Liz had to voice a protest. "Wait a sec! I see two flaws in your scenario. First, Jorge can't be involved in a scheme like that. I know him. He's not just my coworker. He's my friend."

"Harry Johnson was *my* friend," Devlin countered, his jaw tight.

"I'm just saying that Jorge and his wife are good people."

"What's the second flaw?"

"We still don't know for sure Emilio is part of the scheme. We don't even know he was the informant you were supposed to meet that night."

"Maybe not. But as you said, he either lifted the shark's tooth off Martín's body or knows who did."

The harsh edges to his face softened. He shifted on the sofa cushions, his thigh nudging hers.

"That was good work, Moore. Keep it up and we might just have to make you an honorary inductee."

"Into what?"

"Our little fraternity." Sliding a palm around her nape, he tugged her forward for a quick, hard kiss. "I'll drive you back to your place. Then Maggie, Adam and I need to get to work."

The kiss was delicious. The impetus behind it wasn't. Irritated all over again, Liz jerked away from his hold.

"Guess again, cowboy. You're not taking me home and tucking me into bed like a good little girl. I want in on what happens next."

The glint that sprang into his eyes suggested he'd been hoping she'd be more bad than good, but he countered her argument with one of his own.

"What happens next is just grunt work. You need your sleep. You have an early flight tomorrow, don't you?"

He knew damned well she did. And *she* knew he was doing his macho protective thing again, cutting her out of the action in the process.

"I can shave off a few hours. Or reschedule the flight to later in the day."

She figured the last option would make him squirm. The clock was already ticking. He couldn't stay off the rig too long before his absence was noted.

His face took on a stubborn cast and he looked ready to continue the debate when Adam stepped into the breach. "Liz is right. She's too much a part of this for us to shut her out now."

"I agree," Maggie said.

Their combined front forced Devlin to give a reluctant nod. Adam picked it up from there and reeled off a string of pseudonyms.

"As I think you know, Devlin's code name is Rigger. I'm Thunder. Maggie goes by Chameleon."

"Like in the lizard? The one that changes its color to fit its surroundings?"

"Like in the lizard. She's very good at changing colors, by the way."

His wife beamed up at him. "Thank you, my darling."

"We all work—or have worked—in various capacities for a government agency known as OMEGA."

Her mind whirling, Liz drove home through the darkness. Devlin sat silent beside her. He'd insisted on coming along, assuring her he'd find his own way back to the resort. She hadn't argued. She was still trying to absorb everything Adam had revealed. Code names. Undercover agents. OMEGA.

The acronym sounded as ominous as the tasks its operatives were apparently assigned. Liz knew a little about agencies hidden within departments buried in bureaucracies. Her father had retired from the military while she was still in her early teens, but he'd pulled two tours at the Pentagon. He'd rarely talked about his work there. What he didn't say, she now knew from her own military days, spoke volumes. Even today *she* couldn't talk about some of the special ops missions she'd flown.

Still… This stuff was right out of James Bond.

Chewing on her lower lip, she slanted Devlin a quick glance. He'd traded the black Lycra for a pair of shorts and a shirt borrowed from Adam. In the dappled moonlight filtering through the eucalyptus trees, he looked like what he purported to be—a tough, tanned roughneck.

His code name fit him like a second skin. He was an oilman first, an undercover operative second. Or was it the other way around? Liz couldn't separate the two. Idly she wondered if he could.

"You know," she said, breaking the silence, "it might help me understand what you're doing if I knew more than your name, rank and serial number."

"What do you want to know?"

"Where you were born might be a good start. Where you went to school. What you do in your down time. Why you list your brother on your next of kin form instead of, oh, say, a spouse. Little things like that."

"Let's take them in order," he said easily. "I hail from Bartlesville, Oklahoma. Got my undergraduate degree from Oklahoma State, my master's from OU. Down time I usually spend trout fishing with my brother in Colorado or tinkering on the '69 'Vette I've been restoring off and on for years. As for a spouse…"

His tone didn't alter significantly, but Liz caught an echo of old regrets.

"We called it quits just before I started working on the Corvette."

"Bad scene?"

"Could have been worse, I suppose. Time and distance had already numbed most of the hurt. Too many long rotations, too few happy homecomings."

"Didn't you ever consider taking a job ashore?"

"I did more than consider it. I sat behind a desk at corporate headquarters for two years. By that time the marriage was beyond saving."

"No kids?"

"No kids."

"Sounds like a lonely life."

"It is. The divorce rate for oil rig workers is almost as high as it is for military officers." Shifting, he wedged a shoulder against the door and slid an arm along the back of her seat. "What about you and what's-his-name? The sleazy bucket of slime I heard you excoriating the night we met. Why didn't it work for you two?"

"Same problem. Time. Distance. A Malaysian television reporter."

"He told you about her, did he? What a jerk."

She whipped her eyes off the road. "You knew about Bambang?"

"We had you checked out, remember. OMEGA is nothing if not thorough." His teeth flashed in a quick grin. "I didn't get quite that level of detail, though. Is Bambang really her name?"

"It is." Liz could laugh about it. Now. "Appropriate, wouldn't you say?"

His chuckles joined hers. She leaned her head back, feeling his arm warm and hard against her neck.

"I was pretty pissed that night on the beach."

"I kinda got that impression."

"Donny not only dumped me, he cleaned out our joint bank account."

"Sonuvabitch."

"My sentiments exactly. Funny thing is, he's now decided Bambang isn't the right one. I got an e-mail from him earlier tonight. He wants me to drop everything and jump on a plane to Singapore."

"I hope you suggested he take a flying leap."

"I wasn't that polite. Or that verbose."

"Good for you."

She thought about telling him he'd contributed significantly to her terse reply, but decided against it. No sense feeding the man's ego—or scaring him off. Particularly when she wasn't quite sure yet where things were going between them.

"Tell me again what the plan is for tomorrow," she said instead. "I want to make sure I have the sequence right."

Devlin worked his fingers under her hair and made a lazy circle on her neck. The pads were rough, raising little shivers where they rasped against Liz's skin.

"We've already got Riever—my controller at headquarters—checking out Emilio. While he's doing that, Maggie and Adam will use the pretext of chartering Emilio's boat to get up close and personal with him."

"He's scoping out Jorge, too," she murmured, feeling a surge of disloyalty to her friend.

"Yes, he is. We're counting on you to conduct a more-personal inquiry before you make the run out to the patch. Think you can do it without sending up a red flag? If not, Maggie or Adam can."

"I'll do it."

"Good enough. I'll be waiting when you return from the patch to count heads and conduct a visual ID." His fingers lost their gentle touch. "If Jorge or Emilio approaches any of them…"

"Emilio might," Liz said flatly. "Jorge won't."

"U.S. passports go for a big chunk of change in this part of the world. Your friend wouldn't be the first man to get caught up in something he couldn't get out of."

Liz didn't want to think of Jorge or Maria profiting from something so evil. Eduardo Alvarez, on the other hand…

"What about El Tiburón? Who's watching him?"

"He's covered."

She mulled that over for a half mile or so. The Pacific shimmered in the moonlight off to her right. Dead ahead, the lights of Piedras Rojas spilled down the black bulk of the hillside to the cliffs.

"What if Emilio and El Tiburón aren't connected?" she said after a moment. "What if Emilio's in this on his own?"

"Possible but unlikely. Harry rotated off another rig, remember. That suggests the operation involves more than one or two locals."

"True."

She chewed on that while the pinpricks of light grew brighter and closer. Moments later she pulled up under the jacaranda tree and cut the engine.

"My place is just up those stairs."

"I'll see you inside."

Liz hated the relief that rippled through her. Alvarez's two henchmen had really done a job on her nerves. The fact that she might have a line on the item their boss wanted back so badly only added to her jumpiness.

Thankfully, no one sprang out from behind the gnarled tree trunk or lurked under the stairs. She made it to her front door unmolested. Once inside, however, that situation changed dramatically.

Her palm was still slapping against the wall for the light switch when Devlin spun her into his arms. By the time he finished with her mouth and moved to her throat, her heart was pinging against her ribs.

"Any chance you might change your mind about letting me tuck you in?" he asked, nuzzling the soft spot just under her jaw.

She didn't want to make it *too* easy for him. "I have an early flight tomorrow, remember? And you have work to do."

"I'm a fast tucker-inner."

Eight

Devlin was as good as his word. He was fast. Very fast. He waltzed Liz from the front door straight to the bedroom, leaving a trail of discarded clothing along the way. Naked, she sank onto the quilted comforter.

He started to follow her down but she got her knees under her and rose up to meet him. Chest to chest, mouth to mouth, they strained against each other. His hands and mouth and stinging little nips soon had her in a fever of need.

She returned the favor, blazing a line of wet kisses and little love bites from his neck to his chest to his belly. He was as taut as a steel hawser when she took him in her mouth.

Then he pressed her back onto the mattress and

returned the favor. He tongued her sensitive flesh, alternating the strokes with a wicked suction that soon had Liz panting and arching her back.

The blinding speed of her climax took her by surprise. Sensation after sensation spiraled up from her belly, fast and powerful and searing in their intensity. Her last thought before she threw her head back and let them rip through her was that Devlin might be handy to have on hand every night. He was *one heck* of a tucker-inner.

She admitted as much sometime later, after he'd followed her over the edge. They lay sprawled across the bed, legs tangled, hearts pumping, perspiration cooling on their bodies. The taste of him was still on her lips. His head squashed her left breast. His arm was a deadweight across her middle. Idly, Liz played with the short, sun-streaked hair tickling her skin.

"That *was* fast," she remarked. "And pretty damned incredible."

"You won't get any argument from me." Tightening his arm, he drew her closer. "Why do you think I pulled a straight twenty-four-hour shift? My original plan was to wait until a few hours before dawn before slipping away from the rig. I was sorta hoping this might happen."

"Hoping, huh?"

A chuckle rumbled up from his chest, rich and unrepentant. "Okay, praying."

"I got the impression your early arrival surprised Maggie and Adam."

"I got the same impression."

Liz trailed a hand over his neck and shoulders, loving the feel of him. So warm, so solid.

So heavy.

She wiggled a little, trying to shift his weight. "You're smushing me into the mattress."

"I like smushing you." Despite the lazy reply, he eased to the side and propped his head in one hand. "I like it a lot, as a matter of fact. Maybe we should think about more smushing when this is over."

Her heart did a funny little flip, but caution lights started flashing.

"I'm not sure that's a good idea. We both learned the hard way long-distance relationships don't work."

"Could be those weren't the right relationships."

Much as Liz wanted to agree, there was no getting around the reality of their situation. Scooting up against the rickety headboard, she tucked the sheet under her arms.

"I fly charters for a living. You work offshore oil rigs. When you're not secret agenting, that is, which I suspect occurs on a frequent basis. We'd be lucky if we saw each other once every three or four months."

"Aero Baja isn't the only charter service handling the big rigs. We should be able to do better than every few months if we pick our locations."

"Why?" Liz was dead serious now. "What do we have going for us besides good, old-fashioned lust? And why do you think we wouldn't make the same mistakes we made the last time?"

"I'm older. You're certainly wiser. We ought to be able to stir experience in with lust and come up with... With..."

"With what?"

The word *love* stuck in Devlin's throat. It was too soon. Way too soon. If he laid something like that on Liz now, she wouldn't believe him. Hell, *he* could hardly believe the potent combination of worry, hunger and anticipation that had brought him off the rig hours ahead of schedule.

That alone told Devlin he had it bad. That and the fact he had to force himself to leave her, despite all that needed doing between now and dawn.

He'd fudged the truth a little when he'd described the upcoming night's activities as mere grunt work. Out of Liz's hearing, he'd shared a quick aside with Adam and arranged a rendezvous here in town. Together they planned to slip aboard Emilio's boat. Devlin suspected Maggie would insist on accompanying her husband, then argue about who should pull sentry duty while the other two poked around. Either way it looked to be a long night.

"Let's think about it," he suggested as he rolled out of bed. "Maybe we'll come up with the answer by the next time I tuck you in. Sleep well, darlin', and have a safe flight tomorrow."

Liz didn't think she would sleep at all. She figured worry about Jorge and repeated replays of Devlin's parting remarks would keep her awake through most of the night.

She dozed off soon after he left, however, and the next thing she knew dawn was filtering through the shutters. After a stand-up breakfast of coffee, juice and a power bar, she jumped in the Jeep and wove through the still-sleepy streets to the airfield.

Aero Baja's chief mechanic was already there. Zipped into a clean set of coveralls, he was gassing up the Ranger. The familiar stink of aviation fuel hung like a cloud on the hot morning air.

"'Morning, Jorge."

"Good morning, Lizetta." Smiling, he squinted up at the cloudless azure sky. "It is a good day for a run, yes?"

"Looks like. I'll go check weather and file the flight plan."

He had the bird gassed and ready to go when she returned. They fell into their normal ritual, with Liz performing a careful walk-around, Jorge marking off the checklist items as she completed them. They'd progressed from the front-engine coupling to the rear rotor before Liz dragged in a deep breath and launched her casual inquisition.

"I was surprised to hear Emilio is taking charters. I thought he was doing pretty well on his tuna runs."

"You know how it is. One day is good, the next not so good."

"I hear some of the tuna captains supplement their income by running drugs."

"I hear that, as well."

She feigned a surprised innocence. "But not Emilio. Surely he wouldn't get mixed up with something like that…would he?"

Mustache twitching, Jorge worked his mouth from side to side for several seconds. With each passing second, the deadweight in the pit of Liz's stomach grew heavier. Oh, God! Surely Jorge couldn't know of or be involved in drug smuggling. Or worse!

"I do not *think* Emilio would do such a thing," he said after a long moment. "But Maria…"

"Yes?"

"She says her cousin always wishes for more than he has." His burly shoulders lifted in a shrug. "So do we all, eh? Maria wishes for a new refrigerator. My grandson wants this thing called a Gamebox. You save to buy a Sikorsky so you may start your own charter service."

"What about you, Jorge? What do you wish for?"

His mustaches lifted in a wide grin. "I wish to be your chief mechanic."

"You got it," she promised with a ridiculous feeling of relief. She hadn't wormed much out of Jorge, but it was enough to ease the awful burden of suspicion. Whatever his wife's cousin might or might not be up to, it *couldn't* involve the mechanic.

"Let's get the cargo loaded before our passengers arrive."

* * *

She lifted off an hour later with the palletized cargo strapped down and the replacement crew of six buckled into the side-facing web seats.

AM-237 rose up to greet her, looming out of the sea like some mythical creature with the two giant cranes for arms and orange fuel flanges for a tail. Liz had radioed ahead to advise the crane operators she was on final approach so they could swing the monster arms out of the way. They were clear when she swooped in, timed her descent to the rise and fall of the platform and touched down.

The crew members coming off their month-long rotation were lined up on the pipe deck and eager to depart. Liz reviewed the manifest while the quarter-master and his folks unloaded the cargo. Paying close attention to both names and faces, she checked IDs against the computer-generated manifest.

One was an American, on his way home to San Diego. Two were foreign born but had visas granting them entry into the States. The other three planned to head straight for La Paz and connecting international flights to Europe and the Middle East.

Her chest tight, Liz screened the American carefully. Was he a target? Would he make it home safely or disappear somewhere en route, as Devlin's friend had? Would he even make it out of Piedras Rojas?

Devlin had assured her each of the six would have close surveillance on every leg of their journey. Still, Liz had to swallow the warning that hovered in the back of her throat as she watched them strap in.

She was about to climb back into the cockpit and power up when Conrad Wallace heaved his bulk up the ladder and onto the helideck.

"Hey! Liz!"

The brisk breeze off the ocean whipped his thin brown hair around his head like a hyperactive dust mop. Hanging on to the lifeline, the AmMex rep inched his way across the pad. Liz hoped to heck he hadn't decided to make a last-minute run back to dry land. She'd have to recalculate her fuel load and redistribute some weight.

"Almost missed you," he huffed. "I was down in the galley."

Swilling coffee and pontificating to anyone who'd listen, Liz guessed.

"What's up?"

"I need to mail this letter."

"Sorry, the mail pouch is sealed and I've already signed for it."

"I know, I know," Wallace groused. "The mail clerk sent the damned thing up before I got my data together. Just drop this envelope in the mail slot at the terminal."

She took the envelope, noting that it was addressed to some company she'd never heard of with a post office box in La Paz. She wasn't going to risk her license and her livelihood by slipping something through customs, though, even if it came from the company rep.

"I can't just drop it in the mail slot. It'll have to go through security screening."

"Sure, sure. No problem."

"See you next run, Conrad."

Nodding, he waved to the men inside the chopper and backtracked along the lifeline. Liz stuffed the envelope in her leg pocket, strapped in and flipped to the power-up checklist on her kneeboard.

Jorge was waiting when she touched down. Liz left him to secure the aircraft and hefted the mail pouch. Hard on the heels of her passengers, she entered the terminal.

The usual customs official processed them in, assisted by a second official Liz didn't recognize. She stood in line with the others, surreptitiously scanning the room. She knew Devlin was conducting a visual ID, probably via the camera mounted high on one wall. She could feel his eyes on her as she plopped the mail pouch onto the counter.

"Here you are. Oh, and this needs to go with it."

Wallace's letter joined the pouch on the dusty tile. The official gave the envelope a desultory glance.

"*Sí*, I will screen it."

Liz left the six oilmen waiting impatiently while the officials pawed through their bags and checked their papers. Exiting the customs area, she started across the terminal for the café. She'd taken only a few steps when a bent, arthritic woman swathed in layers of black hobbled forward. She clutched a knobby walking stick that tapped out an unsteady beat with each step.

Politely Liz went around her. Or tried to. A clawlike hand reached out and snagged her arm. Startled, she looked down into a seamed face framed by wispy white hair. Bottle-thick glasses magnified the woman's eyes into blurred brown orbs. Her voice weak and wavering with age, she asked for assistance.

"You are pilot, *sí?*"

"*Sí*."

"Would you help me to find my bag? It doesn't come off the plane."

Liz threw a quick glance around the terminal. She wanted to track down Devlin, hear the results of last night's efforts, verify he had a visual on her passengers.

"*Por favor,*" the crone pleaded.

"Yes, of course. Lost baggage is right this way."

At the baggage claim area Liz looked in vain for a handler.

"I don't see…"

The grip on her arm tightened. "In there," the woman murmured in an entirely different voice, thrusting her toward a side door.

"Hey!"

"It's me. Maggie."

Her jaw sagging, Liz gaped at the seamed face.

"In here."

Still slack-jawed, Liz let Maggie tug her into a dusty, disused office. Adam was there, in deep conversation with a slender blonde in a leg cast and a gorgeous Latino. Devlin sat with his shoulders hunched and eyes locked on the screen of a high-tech laptop.

He was in black Lycra again. Her pulse jumping at the sight of all those interesting bulges, Liz skimmed a quick glance around the room. His wet suit and scuba gear were stashed in a corner. Stifling a pang of regret that they'd only have time for another parting, she returned the smile he aimed in her direction.

"Good run out to the patch?"

"Smooth as a baby's butt," she replied.

Her attention diverted, she watched in utter fascination as Maggie straightened and shed a good fifty years with just a simple rearrangement of her features.

"How the heck did you do that?"

Grinning, the brunette slid the bottle-thick glasses down to the tip of her nose. "It's simple. You think old, you act old, you are old. Same when you're playing a giddy young housewife or a tired IBM executive."

"Or a streetwalker," the hunk of a Latino commented, strolling over to join them. "That is how I met Chameleon," he explained, his smile devastating under a pencil-thin black mustache. "In a very dark, very smoky bar. I am Colonel Luis Esteban," he said, offering Liz his hand. "And this is my wife, Dr. Claire Cantwell."

"Code name Cyrene," Maggie supplied as the blonde stumped forward on her half cast. "Luis and Cyrene were supposed to be on their honeymoon. They flew in to help with the surveillance."

"We couldn't let you two have all the fun."

Smiling, Cyrene was about respond to Liz's question about her cast when Devlin scraped his chair back.

"Okay, team. Those six men are the same ones I tagged on the rig. I've activated their tracking devices. Check to see if you're picking up their signals."

The other four flipped up cell phones and punched various buttons. Liz felt distinctly left out when they acknowledged the signals and prepared to disperse. The blonde and her husband, she was informed, would follow the three men heading straight for the La Paz airport and see they boarded their international flights. Adam would trail the American, who had driven down from San Diego and planned to drive back. That left two—a Mexican electrician's helper who lived right here in Piedras Rojas and a Portuguese crane operator.

"You need to keep the Portuguese on your radar screen," Devlin said to Maggie. "He was issued a visa to visit relatives in the States. The visa's good for six months."

"I've got him covered."

Right before their eyes she went through a re-transformation. The glasses slid up, blurring the brilliance of her eyes. The lines of her face seemed to sag. Her shoulders slumped. Grasping the walking stick, she shuffled toward the door.

"What about me?" Liz asked Devlin when the others had departed. "What can I do?"

"You can tell me what Jorge had to say this morning." He checked his watch. "I've got a little time before I need to get back aboard the rig."

"How are you planning to accomplish that in broad daylight without anyone seeing you?"

"Through one of the subsea escape hatches."

She'd forgotten about the safety hatches. Some were designed to allow subs and other submersibles to dock to a rig and perform rescues in a catastrophic event such as a sinking. Others merely allowed crew members to egress the structure and swim like hell.

"What did Jorge say?"

"He said Emilio is always wishing for more than he had."

"Our friend Emilio has more than meets the eye. Adam and I shook down his boat at oh-dark-thirty this morning. He's running a seven-hundred-horsepower Caterpillar diesel turbocharged engine."

Liz whistled softly. "That's a lot of horses for a fishing boat."

"It is. Plus he's packed it with electronics. Radar, a new loran system, GPS—everything he needs to dodge coast guard patrol boats."

"You think he's running drugs?"

"I think it's a damned good possibility."

Devlin's jaw set. The ice in his eyes sent a little shiver down Liz's spine.

"The question I want answered is what else he's running. Adam and I planted hidden cameras. Next time Emilio puts out to sea, OMEGA will be watching. In the meantime…"

The hard edges softened and the cocky roustabout she knew emerged once again.

"In the meantime," he said, slipping an arm around her waist, "let's both do some thinking."

"About?"

He drew her closer, teasing her mouth with his. "What we talked about last night."

Nine

Despite her shuffling gait and sweltering layers of black clothing, Maggie had no difficulty keeping up with Paulo Casimiro. The big, curly haired Portuguese departed the Aero Baja terminal toting a duffel bag on his shoulder and, according to Rigger, a full month's pay in his pocket. His red-and-white-striped shirt made him an easy target. The electronic device Rigger had planted on the man made following him even easier. Maggie hobbled along, dropping well back at times. Other times, she'd hike her heavy black skirt, cut through back alleys and pick him up again when she emerged onto Piedras Rojas' one main street.

Lord, it felt good to be back in the field again!

After ten years of marriage, she adored Adam more than she would have dreamed possible and experienced a ridiculous gush of love at the mere thought of Gillian's cornflower-blue eyes or Samantha's infectious giggles. And Adam Ridgeway Jr. aka the Tank. So sturdy. So strong. Smelling of baby powder and the dirt and their horse of a dog loved to dig in. Maggie missed the kids more with each passing hour, but had to admit being part of the action again sent a sizzle through her veins. Enjoying the adrenaline rush, she kept on her target.

He was booked on a flight out of La Paz tomorrow morning, reportedly heading for Boston to visit relatives before flying home. The man had plenty of time to idle away until then, but appeared to be in no hurry to squander his pay. He strolled down the street, savoring the scent of pork sizzling on charcoal braziers and the raucous salsa beat booming from the corner stand where an enterprising youngster hawked CDs and video games.

He made the mistake of stopping to purchase a CD. Like a Biblical plague, a swarm of other determined entrepreneurs appeared from nowhere, offering outrageous discounts on everything from hand-worked jewelry to hubcaps. The crane operator slapped a thorny palm over his back pocket to avoid losing his wallet and waded through the noisy throng. A determined quartet trailed him for several blocks.

"You come off the rig, yes? You buy tequila or rum to take home."

"This silver is from Taxco. Look, it is very fine workmanship."

"You want a woman, señor? My sister, she is beautiful."

Shaking his head, Casimiro plowed ahead. The eager salesmen dogged his heels.

"My sister, she has a friend. Many friends. You like two women? Three?"

"Taxco silver is the best, señor. Look! Look!"

In an effort to lose them, the Portuguese ducked down a side street. Maggie started to follow but stopped when a figure emerged from the shadow of a doorway. With the rolling gait of those used to a deck under their feet, he sauntered after the roustabout.

"Hola, señor."

Casimiro threw a glance over his shoulder. Mixing Spanish and a smattering of tortured Portuguese, Emilio caught up with him.

"You come off AM-237, *sí?*"

"*Sí.*"

"My friend works the rig." He slapped a hand on the roustabout's back, one deepwater man to another. "I have tequila on my boat. The *Santa Guadalupe*. She is just there, at the dock. I will pour you a drink, yes, and you tell me how my friend does."

Some yards back, Maggie slipped a hand into her skirt pocket. Her heart thumping, she palmed a cell phone. When she raised her hand again, a casual observer would have thought she'd lifted it to scratch the hairy wart on her chin.

"OMEGA control," she murmured into the speaker, "this is Chameleon."

"I'd better make tracks."

Devlin gave Liz a last, long kiss. He'd delayed his return to the rig as long as he dared to hear what she had to say concerning Jorge. He'd also tracked the movements off all six targets. Three were on a bus en route to the La Paz airport, with Cyrene and Esteban right behind them. The local had arrived home and was undoubtedly enjoying a reunion with his wife and kids. The American had picked up his car and hit the road north, with Adam following a few miles behind. Maggie had the Portuguese in her sights.

Much as Devlin hated to depart the scene, he had to get back to the rig. If these six made it home safely, the next six might not. OMEGA intended to keep him in the field until they broke this vicious ring.

Leaving Liz made the departure harder than he'd anticipated, however. The woman was now not only in his head. She was in his blood.

"When are you scheduled to make your next run?" he asked, retrieving his scuba gear.

"AmMex is flying in an on-site inspection team. I'm supposed to haul them out to AM-237 on Wednesday."

"Wednesday, huh? If I'm still on the patch, maybe you can arrange…"

His cell phone pinged, cutting him off in midsentence. Riever was coordinating the movements of all four agents from headquarters. That was his ring tone. Dropping his gear, Devlin flipped up the phone.

"Rigger, here."

"It's Riev. Chameleon's target was just approached by the local you had me check out, Emilio Garcia. She says— Hang on a sec."

Fierce satisfaction ripped through Devlin. Finally! A real break!

"That was Chameleon. She says the target and Garcia boarded his boat and went belowdecks. She's going to slip aboard, as well."

"Adam and I planted cameras on that craft last night," Devlin reminded him with tense urgency. "Get those activated, Riev."

"I'm receiving the visuals as we speak."

Devlin kept the phone to his ear and used the brief pause to fill Liz in. "Emilio lured the Portuguese crane operator aboard his boat. Maggie's going aboard as well."

"I've got Garcia and Casimiro on the screens," Riever reported, switching to broadcast mode to include both Rigger and Maggie on the transmissions. "There's someone else in the cabin. I don't... Hell! Whoever it is just whacked the Portuguese over the head with a marline spike. He went down like a felled ox. Chameleon, did you copy that?"

"I copy. I'm going below."

"No!" Devlin bit out. "Wait for backup."

He was already digging in his gear bag. Retrieving a belt with a lethal assortment of attachments, he raced for the door. A startled Liz chased after him.

"Hang tight, Chameleon. I'm on my way."

"Can't wait," Maggie replied in a terse whisper. "Emilio's firing up the engines as we speak. They'll have to come above deck to throw off the mooring ropes and clear the dock. I'll take them one at a— Uuuuuh!"

The small grunt was followed by silence that sliced into Devlin's heart. Riever broke the stillness with a taut transmission.

"Chameleon, this is control. Come in, please."

Devlin was in full sprint, the phone jammed against his ear. He burst through the rear door of the terminal into a blinding haze of light.

He and Riever weren't the only ones on the net, he discovered as he and Liz ran for the vehicle he'd parked at the rear of the building.

"Chameleon, this is Thunder." His voice as cold and sharp as a scalpel, Adam tried to contact his wife. "Come in, please."

Devlin strained to hear over the hammer of pounding footsteps. Maggie didn't reply. A second later Riever made a stark report.

"We've lost her signal."

"What about the cameras?" Devlin panted into the phone. "Are you still receiving visuals?"

"Roger. I'm showing Emilio at the controls. The other guy is tying up our target. Wait! Here comes a third. He's dragging something behind him. Something bundled in black."

Over the jackhammer beat of his heart, Devlin heard the hiss of Adam's indrawn breath.

"It's Chameleon," Riever confirmed after a second that seemed to stretch for hours. "Looks like she's out cold, but she must be alive. They wouldn't waste rope tying her up otherwise."

The vise around Devlin's heart eased a micrometer. He grabbed the vehicle's door handle and threw the web utility belt in the backseat. Liz jumped into the passenger seat.

"The boat's moving," Riever reported as Devlin jammed the key into the ignition. "We're tracking it via the signals from the device planted on the Portuguese."

Adam came on the net again. His years as head of OMEGA resonated as he assumed command of the situation.

"Notify the coast guard. Mexican or American, whoever's got a cutter nearby. Tell them to run an immediate intercept. And get some air cover. I'm returning to Piedras Rojas. Keep me advised."

Devlin snapped his phone shut. He didn't have time to provide Liz with more than the bare essentials. "They've got Maggie and are putting out to sea. Adam has requested air cover."

She whipped her head up. "We can manage that. Let's go!"

Liz was out of the car and running before Devlin retrieved his utility belt. The Aero Baja chopper sat baking on its pad, right where she'd set it down less than an hour ago.

Her mind churned as she calculated fuel, weight, airspeed and direction on the fly. She hadn't had to buck headwinds on the run out to the patch this morning. The cargo hold was empty. With only her and Devlin's weight to factor into the equation, she should have enough fuel to stay in the air for an hour, if necessary.

Scrambling into the cockpit, she initiated the power-up sequence. Devlin tossed his gear into the rear compartment before releasing the tie-down straps and kicking away the chocks. He scrambled into the copilot's seat just as Jorge erupted from inside the hangar. Swiping his hands on a rag, the mechanic rushed over to the pad.

"Where do you go?" he shouted above the roar of the engines.

Liz weighed the odds and came down firmly on her friend's side. She trusted this man. Besides, there was a lot of ocean out there. OMEGA had lost Maggie's signal. If they lost the signal they'd planted on the Portuguese, Liz might be able to lock on to the fishing boat's transponder or ship-to-shore communications.

"We're going after Emilio," she yelled. "He's just put out to sea with Mrs. Ridgeway aboard."

"Señora Ridgeway charters his boat? He says nothing to us."

Liz didn't have time to explain. "Do you know what RSS frequency Emilio transmits on?"

Devlin had said the fisherman had crammed his boat with electronics. Liz was betting the array included a Ratt Ship/Shore radio, the type used by most ships at sea to transmit and receive administrative and operational traffic. Shore stations transmitted on 5, 10 and 15 megahertz bands. Ships responded on frequencies in the 2, 3, 4, 6, 8, 16 and 22 megahertz range. Liz didn't have time to run through all of them searching for signals from Emilio's radio.

"Jorge, please! Mrs. Ridgeway's in trouble. What frequency?"

"Six-point-five. Sometimes eight-five." His face grim, the mechanic stuffed the rag in his back pocket. "I will come with you to help you look."

Liz darted a glance at Devlin, who gave a curt nod. Once Jorge was aboard and strapped in, the chopper lifted off the pad.

The tracking device Devlin had planted on the Portuguese crane operator continued to transmit, thank God. OMEGA headquarters vectored Liz on a course that took her north by northwest.

Using both hands and feet to work the controls, she pushed her bird to max airspeed. Ten pulse-pounding minutes later they picked up the lighter aquamarine of a boat's wake trailing through the cobalt-blue of the Pacific. Mere moments later they spotted the boat.

"There!"

Leaning over Liz's shoulder, Jorge pointed at the white speck. Devlin had filled him in on the details. He now knew what drove their desperate hunt for his cousin.

"That is the *Guadalupe*."

Nodding, Liz pushed for a few more knots of speed. The white speck grew to a fat-bottomed trawler, churning up a frothy wake. Its twin booms formed a V with the tall mast centered between them. The rear deck sported piles of rolled nets and a hoist that jutted up and out over the deck at a forty-five-degree angle.

"How close can you get me?" Devlin asked, straining forward in his harness to sweep the boat with narrowed eyes.

"As close as you want." Liz lined up on the rocking mast. "Getting you aboard her is another matter. I can skim alongside just above the waterline and let you swim for it or Jorge can lower you to the deck on a sling."

Either way made him an easy target should Emilio and friends object to being boarded. Liz tried to think of another option.

"Try the radio. See if you can raise them. Maybe they'll surrender peacefully if they know we're on to them."

Devlin flipped through the frequencies to six-point-five and keyed the mike. "Ahoy, *Santa Guadalupe*. This is Aero Baja 214. Do you read me?"

They waited for a response, static filling their earphones.

"*Santa Guadalupe*, this is Aero Baja 214. We're right off your stern. Do you read me?"

Liz held the chopper steady as a figure appeared on the back deck and trained binoculars at the fast-approaching chopper. The red handkerchief knotted around his neck gave a good clue as to his identity.

"That looks like Emilio."

"*Sí,*" Jorge confirmed in a low growl. "That is my wife's cousin. *Híbrido!*"

A second figure popped out of the cabin. This one clutched a high-powered rifle. Emilio dropped the binoculars and stabbed a finger at the chopper. His cohort brought the rifle up to his shoulder. So much for a peaceful surrender!

"Hang on!" Liz shouted.

Gripping the collective, she prepared to take evasive action. Before she could jerk the controls, a third individual burst onto the deck. Streaming long white hair, she leaped forward and swung an odd shaped bat.

"That's Maggie!" Devlin strained against his harness. "Jesus! What's she armed with?"

Whatever it was, it caught the shooter up alongside his head. Stunned, the man staggered against the ship's rail. Maggie swung again and sent him careening over the side. His rifle went overboard with him.

She then turned her attention to Emilio, who dived for one of the long-handled gaffers lashed to the rail. With its sharp hook, it made for a lethal weapon.

Maggie fended off his attack with her own weapon while Liz swooped in as close as she dared. The skids were less than a foot off the water when Devlin dived in. Jorge splashed in after him.

Mindful of those rocking booms, Liz had no choice but to back off. Her heart jammed in the middle of her throat, she watched Maggie go down on the slippery deck. She scuttled backward, dodging a vicious swipe of the gaff and scissors kicking wildly to untangle the heavy skirts wrapped around her legs.

Liz didn't stop to think. Helicopters flew every which way but loose. Sideways. Backward. With the right pilot at the controls, they could do a pirouette while maintaining forward momentum. They could even turn on their sides and put out a rotor wash powerful enough to knock a full-grown man off his feet.

Which is exactly what it did.

Flying horizontal with the surface of the sea, Liz caught only a glimpse of Emilio as he hurtled across the deck and slammed into the cabin bulkhead.

Liz trailed the *Santa Guadalupe* back to Piedras Rojas' tiny harbor. She made a low pass, saw Adam standing on the dock and waved to him before zooming in for a landing at the Aero Baja terminal. Once there, she jumped in her Jeep and tore back through town to the harbor.

They were all still aboard the tuna boat, waiting for the Mexican authorities to arrive and take the suspects into custody. Maggie had shed her wig.

Paulo Casimiro was white around the gills, shaken from his near brush with death. Jorge nursed bruised and skinned knuckles, which no doubt accounted for the bloody pulp that used to be his cousin-in-law's nose. Devlin and Adam were conducting similarly physical and very intense conversations with two unidentified males. Sullen and restrained by plastic cuffs at wrists and ankles, the two pointed a figurative finger at Emilio.

"Not that we need their cooperation," Maggie said, combing her fingers through her honey-brown hair. "Emilio admitted he was paid to lure Paulo onto his boat, conk him over the head and steal his papers. The bastard bragged about it, in fact, after he had us trussed up like sardines."

"How did you get loose?"

"An old trick Adam taught me when we were both at OMEGA." Throwing her husband a fond glance, she lifted her skirt and waggled a laced-up granny shoe. "Always tuck a straight edged blade into your sole when you're going into the field."

"I'll remember that."

"Doesn't hurt to have a stuffed mackerel on hand, either." Grinning, Maggie pointed at the object wedged in the corner of the deck. "Emilio had it mounted on the wall inside the cabin. The thing packs quite a wallop."

"A fish? You knocked a couple of thugs on their asses with a *fish?*"

"Nothing special about that." Her brown eyes

sparkled with laughter. "You did the same to Emilio with a whoosh of air."

"Speaking of thugs…" Liz swiveled around to get a better look at the two men hunched beside the tuna boat captain. She didn't recognize either of them. "Do they all work for El Tiburón?"

"Evidently not. Emilio bragged about that, too. Said The Shark wanted nothing to do with the scheme, that it was too risky and would bring police from every country converging on this area. So his nephew, Martín, ran it without his uncle's knowledge. Emilio was one of his captains. Only, they had a slight falling out, which ended with a bullet between Martín Alvarez's eyes."

Liz let out a low whistle. Emilio had stepped in some serious doo-doo. Not only would he have the police coming down on him, he'd have to answer for flouting El Tiburón's authority in his own territory.

She knew which one *she'd* worry most about.

Ten

"We're still missing a key piece of the puzzle."

Devlin deposited his plate on the sturdy trunk Liz used as a coffee table. The remains of their microwave pizza littered the surface.

It was late, well past midnight, but a wide-awake Liz sat cross-legged beside him on the sofa. Still pumped from the wild chase this morning, she'd waited here at her apartment while Devlin and a small, select group of law enforcement officials conducted marathon sessions with Emilio and his cohorts.

The interrogations would continue for some days, but the rest of the OMEGA team had dispersed. Maggie and Adam had left for home. Claire and her new husband had resumed their honeymoon. Devlin would remain in the area a while longer. Although the Mexican authorities had promised to keep his ties to the U.S. Government quiet, he knew the information was bound to leak. Probably already had. He figured he'd blown his cover, but didn't intend to leave until he'd fitted all the pieces together.

"Emilio swears his only contact was Martín Alvarez," he told Liz, reiterating what Maggie had told her on the boat. "Alvarez supplied the names and photos of the targets and told Emilio when they were scheduled to rotate off the rig. He also picked up the papers after Emilio had…had disposed of the bodies."

The words sliced at Devlin's throat like broken glass. He had no doubt now Harry Johnson was dead. Emilio claimed he didn't know Harry, had nothing to do with his disappearance. He probably hadn't, as Devlin's friend had rotated off another rig farther south. Yet Emilio admitted Martín's instructions were explicit. Snatch the target. Take the papers. Weight the body with lead weights and feed it to the fish. He also admitted Martín did business with other boat captains along the coast.

Anxious to cut a deal, Emilio had supplied names of the captains he knew or suspected were part of the scheme. The Mexican authorities were rounding them up and bringing them in for questioning. Devlin planned to be present at the interrogations but he suspected they'd sing the same refrain Emilio had. Their only contact was Martín Alvarez.

"So why did Emilio go after Paulo?" Liz wanted to know. "With Martín dead, he wouldn't get paid for stealing the papers."

"He and Alvarez had set up the snatch before they got crosswise of each other. Emilio went ahead with it, figuring he wouldn't have any trouble coming up with another buyer. He was also hoping Martín's inside man—his source for information about the crew members rotating off the rig—would contact him directly when he learned of the snatch. Turns out Emilio planned to take over operations from Martín. That's why he lifted the shark's tooth off the body, by the way."

"He needed an authority symbol? Something to show he was now in charge?"

"Exactly. He had to be careful where and when he flashed it, though. Martín had warned him his uncle wanted no part of the scheme."

"Emilio-baby took one hell of a chance there." Liz's face screwed into a grimace. "Speaking from personal experience, I can tell you El Tiburón has access to all kinds of information. He would have latched on to Emilio sooner or later."

"We're lucky it was later." A tight knot of anger still twisted Devlin's gut, but he forced a smile. "We can chalk that one up to you. You spotted the shark's tooth and made the connection."

"Did Emilio still have it on him when they booked him?"

"Yeah, he did."

"What do you want to bet it won't remain in the evidence locker for long? The Shark has connections."

"Doesn't matter. We've got Emilio's confession on videotape. We don't have to have the tooth to connect him to Martín or the murder-for-passport scheme."

Frowning, Devlin went back to the missing link, the piece of the puzzle he had yet to find.

"Someone was providing Martín with information about the rig crew members. Names. Nationalities. Rotation dates. Someone with access to the AmMex personnel database."

The woman next to him gave a small hoot. "Their system isn't exactly secure. Any precocious eight-year-old could hack into it. I got in a few times myself to verify passenger data."

"Tell me something I don't know. Our experts found a dozen unauthorized accesses. We also screened thousands of e-mails sent via AmMex's satellite communications system over the past three months. None of them led back to Martín Alvarez."

"So the inside person passed the information to Alvarez by other means. In person, maybe, when he came ashore."

"Or by a message hidden in some object carried off the rig by an unsuspecting mule."

Liz made another noise, this one more of a choking gulp than a hoot.

"What?" Devlin asked.

"I haul a mail pouch out and back on every run."

"I know. Every item you hauled out and back since I arrived at the patch was screened."

"Not every item."

"What do you mean?" His brows snapped together. "Did you act as a private courier for someone on the rig?"

"Do I look stupid?"

Actually, Devlin thought wryly, she looked indignant as hell.

"I don't know most of those guys," she said, skewering him with a glare. "I wouldn't try to slip something through customs even for someone I *did* know. In this country, antics like that can earn you a one-way ticket to a very small, very crowded cell."

"Then what did we miss?"

"Nothing much, really. I probably shouldn't have even brought it up. Conrad Wallace had a letter he wanted to get in the mail, but he'd missed the pouch so I carried it back for him."

"Wallace, huh?"

Devlin turned the information over in his mind. After the AmMex rep had dropped that remark about losing big at the casinos, he'd had OMEGA comb through the man's personal finances. The queries had turned up a few questionable transactions but no major infusions of cash. This letter would most likely turn out to be a dead end, too. Still, it needed checking out.

"What did you do with the letter?"

"I gave it to the customs official at the terminal. I

assume he screened it before he dropped it in the mail slot with the pouch."

"Did you see who it was addressed to?"

"A company in La Paz. Marine Supplies, Incorporated, or something like that."

Devlin extracted his cell phone from the case clipped to his waist. "It's probably nothing, but I'll have our guys check this company and…"

He broke off at the slam of a car door. His glance sliced to Liz.

"Expecting someone?"

"No. You?"

Shaking his head, he pushed off the sofa and slid a hand into the gear bag sitting beside the trunk. His fingers closed around cold steel as footsteps sounded on the stairs, quick and fast. Devlin jerked his chin toward the waist-high divider between the kitchen and the living room.

"Get behind the counter."

Liz gave him a disgusted look and retreated to the kitchen, only to emerge a second later with her fist wrapped around the handle of a kitchen knife.

Devlin didn't have time to argue. Thumbing the safety on the Walther PPK, he planted his shoulder blades against the wall beside the door a half second before their uninvited visitor rapped against the thick panel.

Devlin made a chopping motion, signaling Liz to remain silent. Another knock followed the first. Louder. More insistent.

"Hey! 'Lizabeth!" The shout came through the panel, muffled but distinctly male. "I saw your lights. Open up. It's me. Donny."

Liz's eyes popped. She gawked at Devlin in openmouthed astonishment before reaching for the door latch.

"What the sweet Jesus are you doing here?"

"I got your e-mail." Her former fiancé leaned an elbow on the door frame and cranked his boyish charm up to full power. "Thought if I showed up in person I might convince you to reconsider."

A dimple creased his left cheek. A week ago that lopsided smile might have given Liz pause. Now it made her want to drill a matching dent in his right cheek.

"Not tonight," she said without batting an eye. "Not tomorrow. Not ever."

"Com'on, 'Lizabeth." Still confident, still cocky, he pushed forward and grabbed her arm. "You missed me. You know you missed me."

Stunned by his arrogance, Liz whipped free of his hold. "I did. For a long time. Now I don't."

"Bull. You can't turn it off that fast."

Devlin had heard enough. Shoving the PPK into its holster, he shouldered Liz aside.

"You heard what the lady said. You're history, pal."

The gutless wonder in the doorway blinked in surprise and backed up an involuntary step. Recovering swiftly, he thrust out his jaw.

"Who the hell are you?"

"I'm the man who's going to plant his fist in your face."

Grabbing Carter by the shirtfront, Devlin spun him inside, drew back an arm and let fly. Bone crunched against bone. Blood spurted from his nose. Carter crumpled like a sandbag that had lost its fill and groaned just once before passing out cold.

Liz was seriously annoyed. She couldn't believe Donny had the balls to show up like this. She would have knocked him on his keister herself once she'd recovered from her shock.

"I wanted to do that," she groused to Devlin.

"When he comes to, you can have the next shot."

"I will."

His eyes met hers over Donny's prone body. She saw the fierce satisfaction of a male who's routed a rival and intends to claim the prize. Stepping over Donny, he curled a hand around her nape.

"I hope you're not nursing any residual pangs for this jerk."

"What do you think?"

"I think… Scratch that." His fingers tightened, drawing her closer. "I *know* I want to be part of your life, Liz. We can work this business of separate careers. Make our schedules fit our needs."

"Are you sure?"

His grin appeared and put a stutter in her heart. "You resolved any and all doubts this morning, when you stood your chopper on its tail. I love your courage." He brushed her mouth with his. "Your incredible skill." Another kiss, longer this time. "Then there's your nice, tight ass."

He kissed her again, hard and deep, and it was all she could do to gasp out a suggestion.

"Why don't we continue the inventory inside?"

"Good idea."

He kicked Donny's feet out of the way and went to close the door. A sudden wash of headlights across the courtyard stilled his hand.

"Now who?" Liz muttered as a black Mercedes glided to a halt beside the vehicle Donny must have driven up in. She got her answer a moment later, when a familiar twosome jumped out of the Mercedes and did a quick sweep of the courtyard.

"Uh-oh."

Tensing, Devlin reached for the automatic tucked into his waistband. "Uh-oh what?"

"The ugly one is Short Guy. The gorilla in the lavender shirt and natty shoes is Wingtips. And that," Liz added when another figure exited the rear seat, "is El Tiburón."

Devlin hefted the Walther into plain view. Spitting curses, Short Guy and Wingtips scrambled for their weapons. Their boss stilled them with a swift order and calmly surveyed the two framed in the open doorway.

"There is no need for guns," he called up to them. "I merely wish to speak with you, Ms. Moore."

Devlin answered for her. "She's not talking to anyone until you and your two goons deposit your weapons in the dirt. Slowly. Very slowly."

The Shark shrugged and reached inside his linen sports coat. Using a thumb and index finger, he extracted an automatic and let it drop. His henchmen were too loyal to argue with him, but scowled as they followed his lead.

"May we come up now, Ms. Moore?" Alvarez asked politely.

Liz looked to Devlin for guidance. She wasn't ashamed to admit she was out of her league here.

"You may," he responded for her. "But your friends wait down there."

"As you will."

"No, *patrón!*" Wingtips followed his involuntary outburst with a spate of impassioned Spanish.

"Be quiet! Ms. Moore knows why I am here."

Liz didn't have a clue, but elected not to broadcast her ignorance as The Shark mounted the stairs.

As at their last meeting, he was elegantly dressed in pleated slacks and a dark shirt, paired this time with the linen jacket. The shirt was open down to the second or third button, affording Liz full view of the ivory triangle nestled against his chest hair.

"You got your tooth back!"

"Yes, I did."

"I *knew* it wouldn't remain in the evidence locker for long."

"You were correct."

Unperturbed by the gun barrel Devlin had sighted on the shark's tooth, the mobster reached the top of the stairs and gave the unconscious Donny a curious glance.

"Was this one bothering you, Ms. Moore?"

"You could put it that way."

"You should have told me. I would have taken care of him for you."

"Devlin here took care of him just fine, thank you."

Alvarez turned his black eyes on the OMEGA agent. "So you are Devlin. My sources have relayed interesting reports about your activities this afternoon."

Liz could see Devlin wasn't too thrilled that the mobster had a radar lock on him, but he covered it with a careless shrug.

"My sources have relayed a few interesting reports about you, as well."

"I should imagine they have." Raising fingers tipped by neatly manicured nails, he fondled the gleaming ivory triangle and turned to Liz. "My sources also tell me you are the one who spotted this on that pig Emilio."

"Well…er…"

Liz didn't want to take all the credit. Or blame, as the case may be.

"This is my good luck piece," Alvarez said quietly. "A shark attacked me when I was swimming out beyond the arches. I had only a small knife, but I put out its eye. After much effort, I killed it and dragged it to shore. I was very young at that time and very strong."

He wasn't exactly a ninety-pound weakling now. Liz kept the thought to herself.

"Ever since, this tooth has been… How do you say? My talisman. The sign of my authority. My nephew stole it and used it without my knowledge. I would have strangled him for that with my own hands had Emilio Garcia not deprived me of the pleasure."

She didn't doubt him for a minute.

"Instead," he said with a thin smile, "I must take my vengeance on Emilio, who conspired with my nephew against me."

"He's under police protection," Devlin bit out. "You won't get to him."

"Do you think not?" Alvarez asked politely.

Liz was trying to decide which one of them to put her money on when Donny decided to regain consciousness. Groaning, he struggled up on one elbow and put his other hand to his nose. When it connected, he winced and snorted a froth of blood into his palm. He stared at the gore for a few, disbelieving moments before fury propelled him to his feet.

"You sonuvabitch!" he snarled at Devlin, so beside himself with outrage he ignored the newcomer in their midst. "You broke my nose!"

"You're lucky that's all I broke. Now shut up and get out of my face before I— Oh, well. Never mind."

Donny sank like a stone again, this time from the swift chop Alvarez delivered to the back of his neck.

"He is not wise, this one." Those flat black eyes lifted to Liz. "Do you wish me to dispose of him for you?"

Liz entertained the notion for a second or two.

With a nasty little pang of regret, she stifled the thought. This was Donny, the man she'd once loved. Or thought she had. The suddenness and intensity of her feelings for Devlin were making her wonder if she knew what love was.

"I'll pass on that," she told Alvarez, "but thanks for the offer."

"As you wish." Dismissing Donny with cool disdain, he changed topics. "Those who know me will tell you I pay my debts. As promised, I have wired an electronic transfer to your bank and paid your loan in full."

"What!"

"I also wired the manufacturer. Your helicopter will be delivered next week. A Sikorsky 450L, I believe it is."

Liz got her breath back in a hot, fast rush. "I can't accept a payoff like that! Not from you!"

"The helicopter will arrive next week. What you do with it is your decision."

"I'll tell you what I'll do with it," she fired back. "I'll donate it to the antidrug task force operating in this region and suggest they fly close cover over a certain hacienda just south of there."

A glint of something that looked suspiciously like laughter appeared in Alvarez's dark eyes. "Perhaps we should renegotiate our terms."

Liz now knew how Alice must have felt after tumbling down the rabbit hole. Her ex-fiancée lay in a heap at her feet. The man who'd turned her life and notions of love upside down was nursing skinned knuckles and a 9 mm automatic. And a cold-blooded killer appeared to think she'd just delivered the joke of the century.

Breathing fire, Liz set him straight. "I'm dead serious, Alvarez. If you don't rescind all these wires you sent, you'll have a brand-new 450L buzzing your compound twice a day and three times every night. I'll fly it myself if I have to."

"Very well. I shall instruct the bank to cancel payment on the loan and cancel the delivery order."

He fingered the symbol of his authority again, considering, weighing, deciding.

"I am a man of honor, Ms. Moore. My own brand of honor, to be sure, but honor nevertheless. Perhaps you will accept this as reward for the return of my talisman."

She eyed the crumpled envelope he drew out of his breast pocket with the same suspicion a plump, juicy hen might give a python. "What is it?"

"Something my sister retrieved from a post office box her son had rented. She found the key to the box when she cleaned out Martín's apartment. I think you…" He included Devlin with a gracious nod. "Both of you will find the contents interesting."

Liz took the envelope gingerly and turned it over. The first line of the address leaped up at her.

"Look!" She waved the envelope two inches in front of Devlin's nose. "It's addressed to the company we were just talking about. Marine Supplies, Incorporated."

"Do you know this business?" Alvarez asked. "I do not. Perhaps because it doesn't exist. Or didn't, until my nephew established it via a post office box. I will leave the envelope with you. We shall consider my debt paid, yes?"

If he hadn't been a drug runner and a killer, Liz might have kissed him.

"Paid in full," she assured him.

"*Bueno.* I shall leave you, then." He stepped over Donny again, sparing him only a passing glance. "Are you sure you don't wish me to rid you of this one?"

"I'm sure."

Since Liz's fingerprints and DNA were already all over the envelope, Devlin gave her the honor of opening it. She extracted a bank deposit slip and a handwritten note with instructions for the amount to be deposited.

"Devlin!" Her voice shrill with excitement, Liz waved the note under his nose. "I recognize this scrawl!"

She should. She'd seen it only a week or so ago on a voucher authorizing a five-hundred-dollar advance on her pay.

"It's Wallace's. Conrad Wallace."

"You sure?"

"I'm sure. Wallace is your man," she said with dawning dismay and disgust. "The one providing the targets for Martín."

"That's what it's looking like to me, too."

Devlin's face could have been carved from granite, and his eyes were as cold as death. Liz wouldn't want to be in Wallace's shoes when the two met up again—which could be real soon. Consumed by a fierce, unrelenting urge to wrap her hands around the AmMex rep's neck, Liz posed a question filled with silky menace.

"What do you say we make a midnight run out to AM-237?"

"Sounds good to me. After I make a couple quick calls, we'll get rid of Carter here and head for the airport."

The mention of his name seemed to pull Donny from his second comatose state of the night. He gave a strangled moan and struggled up on one elbow, his expression a study in painful confusion.

"'Lizabeth?"

Shaking his head to clear it, he started to push to his feet. He was halfway up when Devlin moved into his field of vision. His eyes widening in alarm, Donny sank back to the floor.

"Smart move," Devlin said with savage approval. "You'd only end up there again, anyway."

"Who are you? What the hell's going on here?"

"All you need to know is that you're out of the picture, pal. Permanently."

Donny bobbled his head in Liz's direction. Gathering his courage, he curled his lip and sneered up at her.

"So much for all those e-mails about how you'd wait for me as long as it took."

"Funny thing about that. I did wait. I was under the mistaken impression that I loved you." Her gaze lifted to the man standing a few feet away. "Then I met a certain roustabout on a deserted beach. He's given me a whole different perspective on love."

Devlin banked his impatience and fury at Wallace long enough to deliver a swift, hard kiss.

"Hold that thought, darlin'. We'll pick up the discussion right here when we get back from AM-237."

Eleven

Less than two hours later Liz radioed the rig lit up like a Christmas tree in the distance.

"AM-237, this is Aero Baja 214. I'm five miles out and have your lights in view. Request you activate the helideck landing system."

"Roger, 214," the on-duty radio operator responded. "We'll turn on the welcome sign and send up the landing officer and tie-down crew. The duty officer wants to know what's up? Why this late night visit?"

"Tell the DO I'll advise him and the chief engineer when I land."

"Roger that."

Liz switched off the mike, gripped by the rage that had accompanied her across forty miles of black ocean.

"I still can't believe that bastard Wallace. The man acted as if every cent of the payroll came out of his own pocket and complained about any extra expense for the rig. The whole time he was feeding off the blood of his coworkers like a friggin' vampire."

"*I* can't believe we didn't find the account he'd set up in the Grand Caymans," Devlin returned.

He kept his eyes on the lights in the distance and tried to suppress the fury that strained against its chains. He could understand the miss. He didn't like it, but he could understand it. Even after he'd fed Riever the account number on the deposit slip, it had taken OMEGA's supercomputers three runs to trace the convoluted routing back to a U.S. bank account. The name on the account was fictitious, but the handwriting on checks written against that account matched that on the instructions in the envelope. It also matched the signature on a slew of digitized documents Riever had pulled from AmMex computers.

Come morning Riev would request videotapes from the bank, hoping for a shot of Wallace either making or withdrawing funds from the bogus account. A visual would provide another nail in the murdering bastard's coffin.

He'd need a coffin, Devlin thought savagely, ripped apart by memories of his last visit with Harry Johnson's fiancée. Eve and her young son had been so sure big, buff Harry would fill the hole in their lives…and so devastated by his unexplained disappearance.

Devlin clenched his fist, pulling at the skin of his bruised knuckles. He didn't notice the pain. Didn't focus on anything but the lights of the platform dead ahead. Wallace would be lucky if he made it off the patch without a toy bear stuffed down his throat.

"How are you going to handle him?" Liz asked, as if sensing his vicious thoughts.

"I'm hoping to God he puts up a fight," was all Devlin would say.

They lapsed into another silence for the last portion of the flight. Landings were trickier at night, but Liz had made enough of them to put her bird into a hover directly above the pad. Floods bathed the helideck in white light.

Clearly visible in his yellow vest, the landing officer waved her down foot by careful foot while the red-vested tie-down crew huddled behind the protective barriers at the far side of the pad to avoid the rotor blast.

The sea was calm tonight, and the deck appeared stable. Still, Liz had to ride the air currents and touch down just right to catch the deck at the peak of its gentle roll. Devlin had his harness unbuckled almost before the skids touched. Liz didn't want to miss any of the action, but she couldn't just jump out.

"Give me ten minutes," she told him. "I'll power down and secure the aircraft while you brief the duty officer and senior engineer."

"Good enough. I'll meet you on the bridge."

Devlin yanked off his headset and shoved open the

cockpit door. Ducking under the whirling rotors, he headed for the stairs.

Liz turned on the overhead lights and flipped to the power-down checklist on her kneeboard. She was reaching for the first bank of switches when one of the red vests sprang up from his crouch. Bent low to avoid the still rotating blades, he wrenched the passenger door open.

"Hey!" Liz yelled. "Wait until I—"

"Take her back up!"

Her stomach dropped all the way to the drill deck when she saw that it wasn't a tie-down crew man who scrambled into the passenger seat. It was Conrad Wallace, white-faced with desperation.

"Take her back up, Liz."

"The hell I will!"

Thrusting a hand inside the vest he must have lifted from the helipad crew locker, he whipped out a snub-nosed .38 and shouted over the whap of the blades.

"I know what happened this afternoon! On the *Santa Guadalupe*. It came over the marine police radio."

The hand gripping the .38 shook so badly Liz sucked in a razor-edged breath.

"Then I heard you were making an unscheduled run. A night run. Coming to get me. Take her back up, Liz."

She shot a glance out the windshield. Devlin had disappeared down the ladder. He was probably halfway to the elevators. The landing officer and rest of the tie-down crew were standing by, obviously confused. They couldn't see the revolver Wallace kept low in his lap.

"I'll shoot you! I mean it. I don't have anything to lose."

If she took him up, Liz figured he'd shoot her anyway once they touched down on shore. But there was a lot of ocean between the patch and dry land.

With every emergency maneuver and crazy acrobatic stunt she'd ever performed zinging through her mind, she gave the landing officer a thumbs-up to signal that she was lifting off again and dropped her hand to the throttle. The slowly dying engine revved back up to full power.

The change in pitch hit Devlin just as he was about to step into the elevator that would whisk him down to the crew deck. Head cocked, he listened as the engine's whine gathered sound and fury.

"What the hell...?"

The rumble grew to a full-throated roar. Devlin had logged hundreds of hours in choppers, flying out and back from rigs all around the world. He recognized the thunder of a liftoff when he heard it. Cursing, he spun around and sprinted for the ladder.

His head topped the edge of the pad just as the skids left the deck. He spotted Liz in the cockpit. Saw Wallace beside her in the passenger seat. Spitting out another venomous curse, he shot up the last few stairs.

The chopper's nose pitched down. It surged forward, gathering speed. His heart in his throat, Devlin exploded across the pad.

The Ranger cleared the deck. A yawning gap of black appeared between it and the pad. Black night. Black water twelve stories below.

Lunging, Devlin sailed through what seemed like a football field of empty space. One hand met only air. The other slapped metal.

Inside the cockpit, Liz felt the Ranger buck like a bee-stung mustang. The center of gravity shifted. The nose tilted. Forty-four feet of rotor blades tipped sideways and sliced dangerously close to the side of the rig. With a high-pitched scream, Wallace splayed out both hands to keep from being flung out of his seat.

That's what the bastard got for not strapping himself in, Liz thought viciously as she fought to keep her aircraft from going into the drink.

"Don't do it!" the AmMex rep shrieked, struggling to aim the gun in her direction without losing his precarious hold. "Don't take us down! I'll kill you! I swear I'll kill you!"

"I'm *not* taking us down."

She couldn't. Not yet. If the aircraft gyrated out of control... If she crashed into one of the flanges...

With nightmare visions of the Ranger exploding and the entire rig going up in a massive fireball erupting inside her head, she worked the pedals and collective. By the time she'd zoomed out over open water, she had a good idea what caused the drag on her right skid.

It was Devlin. It had to be Devlin. No one else would be insane enough to make that kind of leap.

Wallace reached the same conclusion a few seconds later. Twisting in his seat, he put a shoulder to the cockpit door and wedged it open a few inches.

Wind poured into the cabin and upped Liz's pucker factor yet another notch. Fighting the violent shear, she kept one eye on the altimeter and the other on Wallace. Then he shouldered the door open another few inches and stuck the revolver into the void.

"No! For God's sake, Wallace! Don't!"

Ignoring her frantic shout, he fired. Once. Twice.

"You'll hit the fuel tank, you moron!"

She'd hoped—*prayed*—that would scare him enough to pop back inside the cockpit. Either he didn't hear her over the scream of the wind or his desperation had made him crazy. It didn't matter. Liz wasn't about to let him take another potshot at Devlin.

The bastard had wedged the door open. Big mistake. Huge. Gripping the controls, Liz risked taking her foot off the right pedal long enough to swing it over the center lever.

"This flight is—"

Her boot connected with Wallace's back.

"—terminated!"

She put everything she had into the shove. The AmMex rep slammed against the door, springing it wide open with his weight, and pitched out.

Most people wouldn't survive falling out of a helicopter and smashing into the sea. Fortunately—or unfortunately—for him, Wallace constituted a minority.

Liz and Devlin were waiting when the rig's search-and-rescue crew hauled him back aboard. He stumbled onto the deck with a blanket wrapped around his shoulders, battered and bruised. The sight of Liz and Devlin started him babbling hysterically.

"I didn't know the real reason Martín Alvarez wanted names and photos of crew members rotating off the rigs! I swear, I thought he was just putting the touch on them."

"Yeah, sure."

Devlin wasn't the only one who refused to buy his line. The duty officer, the senior engineer, the search-and-rescue coordinator and a half-dozen roughnecks and roustabouts had all gathered on deck. Word of the AmMex rep's attempt to hijack the Ranger had flooded the patch like an uncapped gusher. Rumor had flamed into fury once the crew learned why.

Wallace knew he'd be lucky to make it off AM-237 in one piece. Panting, wild-eyed, dripping seawater from his nose, he threw a frightened look around the circle of hostile rig workers.

"Those men had just been paid! A whole month's salary. I thought— I was sure Alvarez just wanted to sell them drugs or…or fix them up with whores."

"You lying turd."

That came from the big, beefy Irishman Liz had ferried out to the patch with Devlin. His fists were bunched so tight the knuckles showed white as he shoved his way forward. Jaw locked, he turned to the engineer, who exercised overall responsibility for the rig.

"I'm thinking, sir, that you and Ms. Moore here should go below. Devlin, too, seeing as he's a police officer or something of the sort. The boys and I will be bringing Mr. Wallace along shortly."

The engineer looked to Devlin. His answer was to grip Liz's elbow and steer her toward the elevators. After a brief hesitation, the duty officer stalked across the deck and joined them.

They didn't make the return run to Piedras Rojas until the next morning.

By that time, Devlin had Wallace's full confession on record, and Doc Metwani had repaired most of the damage caused by his private session with the crew. Bruised, battered and cuffed with plastic restraints, Wallace huddled in a mass of shivering misery while Liz went to Devlin's cabin to advise him she had the Ranger gassed and ready to go.

The cabin door was ajar, the lockers open and the built-in shelves empty. Devlin stood beside his desk, his packed gear bag at his feet. His sleek little laptop was shut down and ready to slip into a pocket on the side of the bag. The toy bear that had slouched against the computer sat in the palm of his hand.

The pain in his eyes stirred an ache inside Liz's chest. She knew what caused it. Wallace had admitted that the list of targets he'd provided Martín Alvarez had included Harry Johnson.

"I'm sorry," she said softly.

"Yeah. Me, too."

He stuffed the toy inside his bag before reaching for her. The pain was still there, shadowing his face, as he drew her into his arms.

"You know that thought I told you to hang on to?"

"You think little things like getting hijacked and almost crashing into the sea would make me forget it?"

"I need you to hold on to it a while longer."

"Why?"

"It'll be a few weeks before we can pick up the discussion where we left off. I'll have to work Wallace's extradition and haul him back to States. Then I need to deliver the news about Harry to his fiancée."

Liz swallowed, fighting a sudden hollow feeling in the pit of her stomach. Was this the first of many times they'd have to put their lives on hold? The first of a hundred goodbyes? Would the absences stretch longer and longer? Would Devlin expect her to wait indefinitely, as Donny had?

Well, she'd learned her lesson there. She was done with waiting.

"Tell you what," she said, locking her hands behind his neck. "*I'll* haul you and that piece of garbage back to the States. And I'll go with you to deliver the news to Harry's fiancée, if you'll let me."

"You might want to think twice about that. It won't be easy."

"No, it won't. And it won't be easy turning what we have into something solid and rich and full. But you said it yourself. We can make it work. Combine careers. Pick our locations. Aero Baja isn't the only charter service handling the big rigs. I can fly for anyone—maybe even this organization you work for."

"You could," Devlin agreed. "I know Maggie and Adam will add their endorsement to mine." A smile slipped past the hurt in his eyes, creasing his tanned cheeks. "We'll have to put our heads together and come up with a code name for you."

The certainty swirling inside Liz's heart overflowed until she felt the warmth all through her body. This was right. So very right.

"Just our heads?" she murmured.

His laughter filled her soul. She'd spent all those empty months waiting for Donny. Or so she'd thought. Now she knew it was Devlin she'd been waiting for. Wherever their jobs took them, whatever deep blue seas needed to be crossed, they'd cross them together.

Epilogue

Six months later

It was the perfect spot for a wedding. The Pacific shimmered with a thousand pinpricks of dazzling light. The December sun was kind to the guests who had trooped down from vehicles parked on the road above, bathing them in gentle warmth while tinting the cliffs that thrust out of the sea at the far end of the beach to umber.

Rows of white chairs were set facing the turquoise sea. Subcommandante Riviera sat on the bride's side, stiff and official looking in his uniform. Jorge's wife, Maria and several of their children occupied the seats beside the police inspector. Anita Lopez and most of the regulars from El Poco Lobo filled the rows behind them. After much debate, Liz had extended an invitation to Eduardo Alvarez and his wife. They'd declined—to Liz's relief—indicating they'd be out of the country, but El Tiburón sent a congratulatory message and an offer to use his yacht for the honeymoon, which Liz politely refused.

Maggie and Adam sat on the groom's side with their three children. Coltish, long-legged Gillian had her father's black hair and killer blue eyes. Samantha was a giggling honey-haired brunette with her mother's lively personality. Tank had barreled through the sand immediately upon arrival and made straight for the water, only to be scooped up a second from total immersion by his vigilant father.

The protesting toddler wiggled impatiently in his designated seat beside Nick Jensen and his wife, Mackenzie. Next to them were Claire Cantwell and her husband. Claire's cast had come off months ago, but Luis Esteban still hovered over her as though she were made of the most delicate porcelain. On Claire's other side was a slender, auburn-haired woman who maintained a firm grasp on the hand of a three-year-old. Like Tank, the boy wanted to get to the waves in the worst way.

Devlin had debated whether to invite Eve and her son to the wedding. She insisted the pain of losing Harry had dulled in the long months since his disappearance and professed to feel only joy that Joe

Devlin found Liz while searching for her missing fiancé. Despite her assurances, Devlin thought she looked too thin and pale.

Apparently he was the only one who thought so. Liz's former fiancé had locked on to Eve at the rehearsal dinner last night and didn't appear at all ready to unlock. Devlin had been ready to rearrange Carter's face again when he showed up at the Two Dolphins, but Liz had felt more magnanimous—particularly since Donny had arrived with a check for the last of the funds he'd appropriated from their one-time joint account.

Not that Liz needed the infusion of cash. She'd already expanded her charter service to a fleet of three, with another helicopter on order. She and Devlin had been working the rigs along the California and Baja coasts for the past six months, with Jorge Garcia heading their shore operations. In the process, Devlin had used his cover twice for OMEGA missions—once to bust a ring specializing in the import of human organs for sale to desperate transplant recipients, once to infiltrate a renegade military group based at a San Diego naval base. Liz had provided air support in both operations.

They made a helluva team.

Devlin didn't realize he'd murmured the thought aloud until a mariachi trio hired for the occasion broke into a lively rendition of "Here Comes the Bride" and all eyes turned to the woman being escorted through the row of chairs by her mother and a beaming Jorge, his mustaches waxed to sharp points for the occasion.

"Yeah," his best man muttered over the beat of the music, "you do. Hope I get as lucky one of these days."

"Hope so, too, Riev."

Devlin voiced the words, but his mind, his gaze, his entire being were centered on Liz. She'd let her hair grow these past months, long enough to sweep up in a crown of blond curls banded by fresh flowers. Her dress was a simple sheath of creamy satin that left her shoulders bare. A smile tipped his mouth when he saw her feet were bare as well. Like the night they'd met, right on this very spot.

He took her hands in his, the smile spreading to his heart.

"Hello, darlin'. Ready to make this partnership permanent?"

Her eyes answered for her. Filled with love and laughter, they warmed every corner of Devlin's soul.

"I'm ready, cowboy."

* * * * *

HOTEL MARCHAND

**Four sisters.
A family legacy.
And someone is out to destroy it.**

A captivating new limited continuity, launching June 2006

The most beautiful hotel in New Orleans,
and someone is out to destroy it. But mystery,
danger and some surprising family revelations
and discoveries won't stop the Marchand sisters
from protecting their birthright…
and finding love along the way.

SPECIAL PRICE!

This riveting new saga begins with

In the Dark

by national bestselling author

JUDITH ARNOLD

The party at Hotel Marchand is in full swing when the lights suddenly go out. What does head of security Mac Jensen do first? He's torn between two jobs—protecting the guests at the hotel and keeping the woman he loves safe.

A woman to protect. A hotel to secure. And no idea who's determined to harm them.

On Sale June 2006

If you enjoyed what you just read,
then we've got an offer you can't resist!

Take 2 bestselling
love stories FREE!

Plus get a FREE surprise gift!

**Hidden in the secrets of antiquity,
lies the unimagined truth...**

Introducing

ROGUE
ANGEL

a brand-new line filled with mystery
and suspense, action and adventure,
and a fascinating look into history.

And it all begins with DESTINY.

In a sealed crypt in
France, where the
terrifying legend of
the beast of Gevaudan
begins to unravel,
Annja Creed discovers
a stunning artifact
that will seal her destiny.

*Available every other
month starting
July 2006, wherever
you buy books.*

GOLD
EAGLE
®

GRA1

Page-turning drama…

Exotic, glamorous locations…

Intense emotion and passionate seduction…

Sheikhs, princes and billionaire tycoons…

This summer, may we suggest:

THE SHEIKH'S DISOBEDIENT BRIDE
by Jane Porter

On sale June.

AT THE GREEK TYCOON'S BIDDING
by Cathy Williams

On sale July.

THE ITALIAN MILLIONAIRE'S VIRGIN WIFE

On sale August.

With new titles to choose from every month,
discover a world of romance in our books written
by internationally bestselling authors.

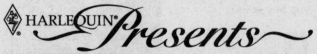

It's the ultimate in quality romance!

Available wherever Harlequin books are sold.

www.eHarlequin.com HPGEN06

Paying the Playboy's Price

(Silhouette Desire #1732)

by

EMILIE ROSE

Juliana Alden is determined to have her last—
her only—fling before settling down. And she's
found the perfect candidate: bachelor Rex Tanner.
He's pure playboy charm…but can she afford
his price?

Trust Fund Affairs: They've just spent a fortune—
the bachelors had better be worth it.

Don't miss the other titles in this series:

EXPOSING THE EXECUTIVE'S SECRETS (July)
BENDING TO THE BACHELOR'S WILL (August)

On sale this June from Silhouette Desire.

*Available wherever books are sold, including most
bookstores, supermarkets, discount stores and drugstores.*

Silhouette® Desire

COMING NEXT MONTH

#1729 HEIRESS BEWARE—Charlene Sands
The Elliotts
She was about to expose her family's darkest secrets, but then she lost her memory and found herself in a stranger's arms.

#1730 SATISFYING LONERGAN'S HONOR—Maureen Child
Summer of Secrets
Their passion had been denied for far too many years. But will secrets of a long-ago summer come between them once more?

#1731 THE SOON-TO-BE-DISINHERITED WIFE—Jennifer Greene
Secret Lives of Society Wives
He didn't know if their romantic entanglement was real, or a ruse in order to secure her multimillion-dollar inheritance.

#1732 PAYING THE PLAYBOY'S PRICE—Emilie Rose
Trust Fund Affairs
Desperate to break free of her good-girl image, this society sweetheart bought herself a bachelor at an auction. But what would her stunt really cost her?

#1733 FORCED TO THE ALTAR—Susan Crosby
Rich and Reclusive
Her only refuge was his dark and secretive home. His only salvation was her acceptance of his proposal.

#1734 A CONVENIENT PROPOSITION—Cindy Gerard
Pregnant and alone, she entered into a marriage of convenience... never imagining her attraction to her new husband would prove so *in*convenient.

SDCNM0506